DARED TO RUN

J. J. Clarke

DARED TO RUN

A Kate Anderson Mystery

J. J. CLARKE

This novel is a work of fiction. Characters, organizations, names and events are a product of the author's imagination or are used fictionally.

The one exception is Chariton County, Missouri. It is an actual place and holds a special place in my heart.

Printed in the United States of America

ISBN: 9781660938520

DEDICATION

To Audrey Anne and Hazel Ann

ACKNOWLEDGEMENTS

I'd like to thank the many people who helped me along this journey, especially my family. I'm grateful for your love and patience.

Thank you to the Writers of the Villages group who have travelled with me while I marched on with a new chapter every week. Your edits and encouragement pushed me forward: Larry Chizak, Dwight Connelly, Richard Domann, Robin Edwards, Jenny Ferns, Ed Fisher, Janis Griffin, Leo Goulden, Jack Grubbs, Bona Hayes, Arthur Huy, Bill Jansen, Millard Johnson, Dee Martin, Barbara Rein, Bob Stowe, Paula Tucker and Dick Walsh.

A special thank you to My Circle of Friends golf group. Your endless support has cheered me on and brightened my frustrating days.

Thank you, Bona Hayes, my editor, who not only put the sparkle in my pages, but also straightened out the gibberish that creeped into the chapters.

We owe our cover and graphic designs to the talents of Josh Lucchesi, who has kept us true to our brand.

We are grateful for the time and talents of Marjorie Speirs, and for her feedback on the manuscript.

And for capturing the scene on the cover, Matthew Anderson. See his beautiful pictures of Missouri at Andersonphotography.com.

Table of Contents

She stood in the storm,
and when the wind did not blow her way,
she adjusted her sails.

— *Elizabeth Edwards*

PROLOGUE

KATE

I bloodied my first nose when I was five years old. A six-year-old boy grabbed my arm and yanked me across the street. When he faced me again, yelling, "Come on," I drew my small-knuckled fist and launched myself at him. I punched him as hard as I could—right in the nose. He whelped and blood spurted everywhere. I looked at my bloodied red fist in shock. A second, bigger boy grabbed my wrist.

"Let me go," I hollered and sat down like a Missouri mule. He tried to yank me to my feet, and I kicked him once in the shin and again, higher. The tip of my blue Converse tennis shoe struck him in the right place. He buckled, clutched himself in pain, and fell to the ground moaning.

A third boy, my friend Johnny, grabbed my ponytail and swung me around to face him. My fist landed on his fat, dark nose. Unflinching, he punched me in the gut. I bent over, head down, and charged his mid-section. We rolled around on the ground and he landed on top, pinning me down with his legs across my chest.

1

His face was inches from mine. "Say, 'Uncle.' Say 'Uncle', or I'll punch you in the face. You're a stinkin' girl. Stay inside!"

Pops lifted Johnny off me, grabbing him by his shirt collar and dumping him into the street. "Enough, boys. Get the hell out of here—you—gutter rats."

The boys ran down the street. I gasped for air and sat up. Tears fell down my cheeks onto my white t-shirt.

Pops leaned down, pulled me up by my elbow, and looked me straight in the eye. "Don't cry, Katrina. There's nothing to cry about, it was a little street fight. Don't you ever let boys drag you somewhere you don't want to go. Do you hear me? Scream, kick, fight—a bit harder next time, Katrina. Fight like your life depended on it. Those boys will *always* be bigger and stronger than you. *You will need to be fiercer and smarter.* Do you understand?"

"Yes sir." Tears fell. I couldn't stop them.

My step-grandmother came out of the house, her beehive hairdo freshly sprayed by her faithful hairdresser. "Young lady, get in the house, take a bath and wash your hair. We're going to have a peaceful dinner—*yours* in your room. Theodore, make me my cocktail."

I burst into tears again and ran down the hall. The screen door slammed behind me. I dove into the bathroom, shut the door and sat against it. I looked at my skinned knees and wiped grimy tears across my dirty face. "I hate boys. I hate boys."

Don't ever let boys drag you somewhere you don't want to go. The thought echoed in my brain and melted into my heart like a mantra. The neighborhood was filled with boys.

I became good at making boys' noses bleed.

CHAPTER ONE

FIREARMS TRAINING

FBI Firearms Training – Limo, Missouri
September 2008 – Twenty Years Later

T en FBI agents, dressed in khaki pants and navy shirts, stood flat-footed at the firing line. Each agent held a black Glock with twelve rounds in the magazine.

"Fire!" the instructor yelled.

The two non-FBI agents sat on the sidelines. Robert O'Dell, a deputy sheriff from the Jefferson County Sheriff's Office, wore brown pants and shirt. He sat next to Kate Anderson, a bond investigator from Missouri Probation and Parole, in black cargo pants and a red polo shirt.

"Is *your* form like that? Don't you think that's weird?" Kate asked Robert.

The firing stopped. Kate said, "That's not how I was taught, but they're all great shots. Look at their patterns, they're dead on. Center mass, tight pattern—that guy on the far left almost shot a perfect hole through his silhouette's heart."

"It's called 'cup and saucer' style. The feds burn ammo several times a week. You'd be good, too, with practice."

Kate elbowed him and tilted her head coyly. "I'm already good. Pay attention to your own target." Her dark ponytail fell down the front of her shirt.

"Pretty confident, aren't you, little lady?" Robert moved closer to Kate.

"I grew up with guns. It got me here—in this advanced class—not that I really wanted to come. I don't think probation officers have any business carrying a weapon. I sit in court or interview inmates at the jail most of the day." Kate, a new college grad in her first job, had been recommended for the elite team training at the FBI Academy. *Will they turn me into a trained killer?*

The instructor, wearing camo fatigues, approached the bench. "Okay, you two, show us what you've got."

The FBI agents walked over carrying their targets. They sat on the long bench, joked among themselves about their scores, and ignored the two stepping up to the line.

Kate strode over to the range and took the end spot. She placed her custom ear protector over her head, draping it like a necklace for a moment. She loved new technology, and this was the latest equipment. It muffled the shots, but also amplified speech.

She twisted the knob on the volume control so she could hear commands and positioned the protector over both ears, then assumed a defensive stance, her right foot slightly in front of her left for balance. She steadied her Smith and Wesson revolver down low—two- handed, thumb over thumb.

Robert moved to the spot next to her and mimicked her stance.

"You *could* move down one," Kate said.

He removed his small ear plug. "Nope, I'm putting as much pressure on you as I can. You gonna talk or you gonna shoot?"

"Suit yourself, tough guy." Kate raised her weapon and pointed at the target.

The instructor yelled, "Fire at will!"

Kate blasted the first round of shots with her revolver. She aimed carefully and hit center mass six times. O'Dell shot twelve times with his semi-automatic Glock. Kate reloaded as Robert watched carefully, then shot six more rounds.

The instructor approached. "The next set are the moving targets. Anderson, with your revolver, you might as well be first. Head toward the barn. If you fail, you go home."

Kate studied the problem. Her heart pounded and she was winded from the adrenaline from firing on the range. *Just don't shoot an old-lady target.*

Kate crossed the field, slow and steady, her weapon pointed down. She chose a barrel for cover. The first target swung up on a spring and startled her. She raised her weapon and pointed, but did not shoot. It was a little girl with a doll.

That's one, should be at least five more. She headed for the next barrel and ducked behind it. The target sprung to life, a brute of a man with a butcher knife raised above his head. Kate shot twice—double tapped as trained. Her first shot struck the man in the throat and the second nailed him in the groin.

"Call 911. Civilian needs assistance. Call 911." Kate's strong voice echoed in the field.

The instructor yelled over the megaphone, "Not center mass, but the target's down. Speed it up Anderson, we don't have all day." Kate heard the group laughing in the background.

She entered the barn, her eyes adjusting to the darkness, hiding behind a wheelbarrow and adding two bullets to her revolver.

This is where it gets good. She moved through the barn and saw a dummy dressed as a police officer on the other side of the barn, his clothes covered with fake blood. She knew exactly what she was supposed to do. Spotting the stairs to the loft, she holstered her weapon, carefully climbed the steps, and belly-crawled across the barn, deliberately avoiding all the bad guys on springs, before exiting out the window and dropping down next to the dummy officer.

Shouting, "Call 911, officer down," she dragged the officer behind a tractor and rang the bell to signal the assignment completed.

She was returning to the group, when the instructor met her midfield. "Anderson, what was your assignment?"

"Assist an officer down, sir. Avoid conflict and confrontation. Missouri Probation and Parole guidelines allow me to fire my weapon only if attacked."

7

"You didn't confront the perps in the barn. Y'all want to be called law enforcement, but you don't want to get your hands dirty."

Kate stood straight and tall. She removed her headphones and looked him in the eyes. "I don't make policy, sir."

"If it were up to me, you'd go home."

"Yes, sir."

The group returned to the beginning and O'Dell ran from behind the barrel, shooting his way through the barn. He shot the three bad guys Kate had avoided. The child and the old lady were unharmed.

The instructor clicked his stopwatch. "Good job, O'Dell. You may have set a new record."

∾ ∾ ∾

After they sat through a boring legal liability class in the afternoon, the trainees were dismissed to a motel pool party. Buckets filled with ice and beer were set up near the pool, and barbecue sliders, fried tater wedges, and wings filled a table under the canopy. Kate wore a conservative navy Nike lifeguard suit. The two other women in the class wore bikinis. Kate noticed two good-looking FBI men, bare-chested and wearing swim trunks, checking her out. She headed to the beer bucket, tiptoeing in the overflow drain along the edge of the pool.

Deputy O'Dell, still fully clothed, came from behind her and scooped her up as if she were a child. Kate

8

grabbed him in a head lock, kicked her feet, and yelled, "Let me go. Let me go."

A bikini-clad agent pushed him from behind, and both Kate and Robert fell into the pool. Robert broke her fall as they hit the bottom in the shallow end and Kate yanked his ear before letting go. She came up laughing, splashed him, then slid through the water, and jumped up and out. She grabbed her towel and sat down in a pool chair.

The crowd laughed, stared, and watched Robert crawl out of the pool fully clothed and drenched.

An agent yelled, "Let's get this party started!"

Robert walked over and sat next to Kate. "I'm sorry, I wasn't really going to dump you in."

"The hell you weren't." Kate laughed. *This guy is trouble.*

"Let me take you to dinner—you had a hell of a first day." Robert sat next to her, dripping wet, his blond hair hanging down his face. His blue eyes twinkled through the splinter of gold.

"Towels over there." Kate pointed to the stack of pool towels. "No thanks on the dinner, I'm hanging out here for a bit. Unlike you, Golden Boy, I may get sent home tomorrow."

"I'll come back and join you," he grinned. "Nice work today." He walked off, his boots sloshing.

She turned and watched him leave. "Suit yourself, tough guy."

∽ ∽ ∽

Kate drank her beer and talked to the two women in bikinis. They rummaged in their bags and exchanged business cards as they all nibbled on appetizers. When the sun began to dissolve into shades of pink against the blue sky, Kate wanted a hot shower—and a chat with Susie, her friend from college. She headed back to her room, taking a short cut through an alleyway.

She stopped once. *Is someone following me*? Goose bumps crept up her arms as she shivered into her hotel room, where she locked and bolted the door, then leaned against it, and slid to the floor. Her legs were trembling. She grabbed her jacket off the bed and covered up with it.

Scrolling through the contacts on her phone, Kate pushed Susie's number.

Susie answered the phone. "Hey girl, how's it going in deep south Missouri?"

"You know, it's *really* different here. Lots and lots of food, I mean it's crazy. I stopped at this place called Lambert's to eat. They just kept bringing side dishes and heaping food on my plate—fried potatoes, okra, hush puppies. Then, this guy with a chef's hat threw a roll at me."

"You're kidding."

"No, I'm not kidding. I caught mine first try, but some people didn't catch them. What a waste— delicious homemade rolls on the floor. It was fun. I wanted to fill my purse."

"Carbs—you'll be sorry when you can't get into your size-four pants. Any cute guys at FBI firearms training?"

"Oh yeah, sure, but Susie, there's this one guy here." Kate sat at the desk and doodled on a hotel message pad.

"Spill it, go on, spill."

"Well, have you ever met a guy that you just felt out of control with?"

"Wow, Kate, I've never heard you talk this way before. Is he the one?"

"Don't be sarcastic, but, no. The opposite of 'the one.' This guy makes me feel unsafe. Wild, crazy, unsafe, heart-stopping, legs-shaking terror to be near him."

"Sounds like love to me."

"No, I'm serious, I'm out of my league here. He's gorgeous, but dangerous—*crazy* dangerous. And, I don't want it to happen, but it's like, I can't make it stop."

"Wow, Kate, you're shook up, aren't you?"

"Yeah, I am. I'm thinking about going home. What am I doing here, Susie? Everyone has an advantage because they have double the rounds in their guns. Why didn't I buy a Glock?"

"Quit? Kate Anderson—quit? You didn't buy a Glock because it's not one of the state-approved weapons. And . . . this isn't about the weapon."

"No, it's about this guy. I'm scared and excited and I wish you were here." Kate put her hand on her forehead.

"Crap, Kate, I don't know. Maybe you're overthinking it. Have some fun. He's a cop, right? He must be normal—well *semi*-normal. Just try to have some fun, Kate."

"I'm fun. I'm *so* fun. I'm dressing right now to have some fun. Besides, it was probably just the adrenaline rush. I get why people are adrenaline junkies."

≼   ≼   ≼

Kate didn't dress to go out. She decided to go for a run. She put on running shorts and shoes and stuck her ball cap on her head. After locking the motel room, she ran across the parking lot and down the road. She picked up speed and crossed the street into a nearby park with bad lighting.

What was I thinking, going on this run? I've made myself a perfect target.

Footsteps sounded behind her and she immediately pivoted to face her opponent. Her hands were raised in fists, ready for a fight.

"Whoa, beautiful, it's just me."

Kate's heart pounded. "O'Dell, what are *you* doing here?"

CHAPTER TWO

TRAINING DUO

Highway Patrol Headquarters
Jefferson City, Missouri - October 2008

T he room overflowed with new recruits from Missouri Highway Patrol and Probation, seated in plastic chairs behind small cafeteria tables. Kate, drafted to teach basic safety skills, waited for the Legal Liability Instructor to finish. Kate's class, Verbal Judo, was based on a training class she had attended in Jacksonville, Florida a few weeks earlier.

The highway patrol group, referred to as "Boots" to remind them they were boot-camp-level trainees, wore basic blue shirts stamped "Highway Patrol" in large white letters. They sat straight in their chairs in the front of the room. Instructors had been yelling at them for two weeks. The Boots met height and weight specifications, adhered to conservative haircuts, and had no facial hair.

Kate's colleagues, Missouri Probation and Parole new hires, were a stark contrast. Every shape of body and style of dress—from geek to hippie—sat in the back of the room. She called this group "Brats," as if they were annoying children, ironic because just a couple of years ago, she had been one of them.

Kate strode into the classroom, wearing black fatigue pants, boots, and a red polo shirt. "Boots! Atten-hut!"

The Highway Patrol group slid out of their chairs and stood at attention. She scanned the trainees from parole services, and one stood out like an elephant in the back of the room. Reese Matthews, her new boss, sat tall in his chair which for him was a size too small.

Kate paced the room and casually placed the microphone to her lips as she talked.

"Be seated." Once the Boots sat back down, she announced, "Your classes have been running late all day. New recruits get overtime at five o'clock. I've been instructed to dismiss on time. Therefore, no questions— save them until tomorrow."

She paused. "What's the point of Command Presence, the first segment of Verbal Judo? Someone know?"

Kate did not wait for an answer. "The ability to project yourself as the one in authority." She set the microphone down and instead projected her strong voice. "If you want to shout out orders and have people obey, you must look like you mean business. You can't look like a hippie." Kate paused in front of a man wearing a tie-dyed t-shirt. "You need to email your supervisor and pick up the dress code." She glanced up and addressed Matthews. "Sir, you—big guy in the back of the room, would you stand up?"

Heads turned, eyes followed, as the entire class spotted the large man.

Matthews stuck a toothpick in the side of his jaw as he stood.

"Now this guy, what? Is he six-one, maybe six-two? Weighs, well—let's say he's not scrawny. He has an advantage, his size. But look how he's dressed, khaki pants and blue blazer, he looks like a cop. He's not, he's a parole supervisor. He's dressed like this on purpose. And, I know you doubt me, but this same guy—with a little help from my girlfriend—could be transformed into a giant teddy bear, all warm and cuddly, harmless.

The class laughed, but Matthews stared down at them. The group looked away, avoiding his gaze.

"Note that stare. I call it the stink eye. He appears like he intends to throw you across the room, and he does it without saying a word." Kate paused. "Thank you, Mr. Matthews—you've been a great sport."

Matthews squinted at Kate but sat down. She continued, "I'll admit, I don't have my dirty look perfected, but my verbal skills have improved." She checked her audience—she was losing them. It was late afternoon on Thursday and the students slouched in their chairs, most yawning. Eyelids drooped.

She placed the microphone to her lips again. "I'd like to introduce my colleague and friend from Kansas City, Susie JONES!"

Susie walked on stage like a model walking onto a runway. Her long blonde ringlet hair stayed in place. She was dressed in a pink polka-dotted skirt, 1960's style, paired with matching pink four-inch heels. At stage center she stopped, looked around the room, then slowly, dramatically, placed a long piece of gum in her

15

mouth. Crossing the stage to where Kate stood, she took the microphone, leaned over the crowd, and showed a little peak-a-boo cleavage. She whispered in a little Minnie Mouse voice , "Boots, stand up."

The entire class stared. No one moved.

Kate took the microphone from Susie. "'Command Presence'—get some! Think about your attire, check the mirror. How will you present yourself? Stand tall. If you *appear* like a victim, you'll *be* a victim. This is a serious job. Look like you mean business—not like you crawled out of bed in your pajamas. Memorize your handout. You'll be sorry if you don't. You're gonna be on camera tomorrow." Kate glanced at her watch. "Five o'clock. Class dismissed."

Kate strode over to Susie. "Thanks for coming. Let's get the hell out of here. That big guy is my new boss."

"You mean the sexy one over there? He's your new boss?" Susie turned and watched for Reese.

Kate pulled her through the hall and out the side door. They jumped into Susie's Missouri state-issued Jeep Wrangler. "Yep, he's my new boss."

◈   ◈   ◈

Once they made their fast getaway, Kate laughed. "I can't believe your boss let you drive all the way from Kansas City for your cameo appearance."

"Well, I didn't tell her I was going to be on stage for a minute, Kate darling. We're salt and pepper. You can't do these productions without me—especially if that damn Robert O'Dell might be in the area." Susie sped the couple blocks to the Best Western Hotel. Kate braced herself as they veered around the corner.

"I may have to start teaching without you. New orders this afternoon. I have a grueling class schedule for the next six weeks. The Verbal Judo course is the new tool and they want me to train all staff. The department must be going through some big procedure modifications. That's why Matthews was in my class."

Kate looked at Susie. "You gonna change before we eat?"

"Of course, Kate."

"Well, don't take all night okay? I'm hungry. There's a bar attached to the hotel—let's meet there. I could use a drink."

"Don't bark your orders at me, sister. It's not my fault your sexy new boss is your type, and not some old guy ready to retire."

"I don't have a type, but yes, it's inconvenient. I like my bosses old and uninteresting. I hope he's not in my class tomorrow."

"Well, *I* hope he's in the bar tonight. Wear something sexy, Kate. Don't show up in those military fatigues. Really, I can't believe you wore them when you didn't have to."

Kate opened the door to the vehicle and flashed her middle finger back at Susie. "Meet you at the bar."

Susie laughed. "I booked an adjoining room to yours, so pick out something nice to wear or I'll come in there and dress you. Wait up. We might as well walk together."

જ   જ   જ

O'Dell sat behind the wheel of his maroon pickup truck a block from Kate's house in Kingseat. His newly cropped reddish hair could not be seen underneath his deputy sheriff's cap. A camo shirt stretched across his broad chest. He cracked a Budweiser and crunched on pork rinds. Swigging his beer, he picked up his binoculars and watched Kate's windows. He checked his watch—just after ten.

She should be home by now. Where in the hell is she?

Robert spotted a Kingseat police car as it pulled around the corner and stopped beside him, window to window. Officer Ron Davis pressed his window button down.

"Good evening, Deputy, you on a stakeout tonight?"

"Nope, beautiful night, just a little R&R. You got a problem, Davis?" O'Dell glared at the police officer.

"Not me, but the brass wants you to move along. Kate Anderson's made a complaint about you watching her. You don't want to get on the wrong side of the police chief."

O'Dell leaned out the window. "I don't give a fuck about your chief."

Davis laughed. "Me either, dude, but you're wasting your time tonight. She ain't coming home."

"Really? How come?"

"She's in a training session in Jeff City. I don't get it, O'Dell. There are plenty of fishees in the sea, why don't you go out and get you one of them? Somebody who'll appreciate your special attention." The police officer snapped finger to thumb. "Here, fishy, fishy."

"Mind your own damn business."

"Calm down, I'm just trying to give my colleague a solid. No need for you to be here if she's not around. The chief's been on my ass about you stalking this girl. Let me tell him I have it handled."

"What time do you get off tonight, Davis? Can I buy you a beer?"

"Thanks, not tonight." Davis put his car in reverse and pulled out of the parking place.

O'Dell drank the last of his beer. *Ass wipe. Like I don't know you're her protector. At shift change, I'll come back and bug her house.*

CHAPTER THREE

GIRLS JUST WANNA HAVE FUN!

Reese sat at the bar at the Best Western and ordered Jamison on ice. He faced the bartender and assessed the two women reflected in the mirror. *They look like college students. "Command Presence" my ass.*

Reese had married his high school sweetheart, served in the army, finished college and begun work with the State of Missouri as a parole officer. His new promotion, jumping many senior officers with more experience, left him at odds with his peers. That discomfort and his recent divorce and relocation, not to mention being forced to attend basic training, had him in a dark mood—except for his interest in the two women.

He sipped his drink and as the warm liquid spread, relaxed and leaned against the wall to watch them. They were engrossed in girl talk. Kate held her head close to Susie's as she whispered. Matthews tried listening but couldn't catch any of the conversation. He ordered another drink. *I'll give it to Kate Anderson, she got everyone's attention.*

He ambled over to Kate and Susie's table and leaned toward Susie as he spoke. "You ladies mind if I join you?"

Susie patted the booth next to her. "Have a seat, cowboy."

"Wasn't planning on working tonight, Boss," Kate said.

"A little spitty, aren't ya?" Reese said.

Kate laughed and stuck her hand out to shake, "Spitty, yep! Get used to it. I'm Kate Anderson, your bond investigator—probably your worst nightmare. I technically work out of your district, but my office is at the courthouse. And oh, the Judge thinks I work for him."

Reese's eyebrows shot up. "Nice to meet you, Kate." He shook her hand. "You're right, I'm your boss. How'd ya know? I just found out myself."

"I have my sources."

Susie moved closer to him. "Pleased to meet you, Reese." Her big blue eyes met his and held his as she crossed her legs and pointed a ballerina slipper in his direction, almost rubbing his leg. "Rule number one, we're not working tonight, so you two can't talk shop. Rule number two, unless you're planning to buy us a drink—or dinner—shove off, handsome."

Reese threw his head back and laughed. "You ladies are straight-shooters, aren't you?" He motioned for the bartender who hustled over to the table, wiping his hands on his apron.

"Continue with the margaritas, ladies?" The bartender looked at Susie.

Susie nodded. "'Tequila makes our clothes fall off'— right?"

The bartender winked at Susie, then addressed Reese. "Sir, your tab, I assume?"

"My tab and let's get a combo platter of appetizers. That work for you ladies?"

"That'll work, for now," Susie said.

"I accept your terms, no job talk. What were you ladies talking about when I interrupted?"

"None of your business, Boss," Kate said. "Susie, what do you think? Should I tell him? It's time for me to look for a bigger and better job."

Reese leaned over closer to Kate. "Scared of your new boss, missy?"

Susie interrupted. "You two are like alley cats. We were thinking about bar hopping, but as you know, Reese," Susie patted his shoulder, "we have an early class tomorrow. Kate has to yell during her next presentation. It's hard when she's hung over."

"Just because the teacher turns in early, doesn't mean we have to." He put his arm around the back of the booth and turned to Kate. "Let's leave any sparring at the office or the gym—where we get paid. I plan to be the best boss you've ever had." He swiveled again and turned his full attention to Susie. "You keep me on the right path, all right, Susie?"

Kate rolled her eyes. "Excuse me, I'll let you two work it out. I see a music player over there—I'll plug it while you talk. Of course, the old timer probably calls it a jukebox or something like that." Kate touched Susie's arm, leaned down, and whispered in her ear. "Don't tell him anything, Susie." Kate's cowboy boots clicked while she walked across the room.

"Don't mind her, she'll get in a better mood after the tequila sets in and she cranks her music. Kate and I went to Southeast together. When we graduated, I took a paralegal position, but she convinced me this new Bond Investigator gig would be fun. The pay stinks, but it has great training, with travel." Susie smiled at Reese.

"I didn't know much about the program until I interviewed for the supervisor job. I've been working here in Jeff City the past couple of years. Didn't it start with the over-crowding in the Jackson County jail in Kansas City?" he asked.

"Yeah, but boring, boring . . . you married, Reese, got kids?"

"Yes—I mean no, divorce was final two weeks ago."

"So, that's why you have a chip on your shoulder? Give us time and maybe we can knock that chip off."

Kate returned to the booth and grinned. "Hey Suze—tell Boss man why I call you Susie Commando."

"Kate, you make me blush." She put her hands to her face, then grabbed a napkin and fanned herself.

"Aww—go on, Susie. He's two whiskeys in, with more comin'. He'll never remember it."

"Well," Susie said, leaning over to Reese and exposing a little pink bow on her bra. "Sometimes—when I wear my red suit to work—I go commando."

Reese looked at Kate. "I don't get it, give me a clue."

"C'mon, Reese, you can picture it, she wears her red suit and four-inch spike heels. She always wears her hair up, all sixties sexy secretary, with some librarian glasses. Only one thing's missing—panties."

Reese locked eyes with Susie as she said, "That's right, cowboy, no panties."

Reese sat back in the booth. "You're kidding."

"Hell yes, I'm kidding. What's wrong with you? You old perv!" Susie slapped him on the back while they laughed. "Or am I? Gets their attention every time—doesn't it, Kate?"

He shook his head, laughed, and downed the rest of his drink.

"We're dancing—this is our song." Kate and Susie left the booth mouthing the words, "Run, run, run away" as the song played.

He watched the two beautiful women dance in the middle of the floor—Kate in a dark French braid, Susie's blonde hair swinging side to side.

❧   ❧   ❧

Reese bought them all dinner, then kept ordering drinks until midnight when just like Cinderella, Kate announced she had to leave the party. Susie followed, blowing Reese kisses as she left.

He finished his final whiskey and threw the bartender a twenty-dollar tip. "Thanks for the great service."

"Thank you, sir. I'll give you a heads-up. You might steer clear of the brown-eyed maiden."

"How come?"

"Bartenders hear things. This I saw with my own eyes. She came in here after training one night. Someone had given her a big shiner. The whole side of her face was black and blue. She wore long sleeves. I could tell from the way she held herself she'd been manhandled. She's got herself a real jealous boyfriend."

Reese slid off the bar stool and grabbed the bartender by the front of his shirt and pulled him across the slick surface. "Gimme a name."

CHAPTER FOUR

BIZARRO

K ate drove into Kingseat just before dark. While her friends from high school pulled through McDonald's with a kid or two in the backseat, she led this life—with criminals and guns. She fingered the Smith and Wesson pistol laying on the front seat, as she studied every passing car, every parked vehicle as a threat. She checked and rechecked her rearview mirror to make sure no one was following.

In the two years Kate had worked for the agency, it had been in a constant upheaval about whether parole officers should carry guns. Kate stood on the side of "no guns, no badges."

What would I ever do without Susie? Kate relived the fight they had after Kate used their code word "umbrella." Susie threw her purse across the sparse hotel room onto the second bed in a dramatic effort to get her point across. "How dare you use our code word after you let me believe I had the go-ahead with Reese?"

"You're not gonna screw my boss," Kate yelled.

Susie put her hands on her hips and glared at her. "Why the bloody not?"

26

"Could we not go into Brit speak? What if he goes all googly eyes for you, constantly asks about you? It's all too damn confusing. Don't I have enough going on?"

"Then stay out of victim-land. You didn't do anything wrong, Kate. You didn't ask to get knocked around. Just because you've had one bad experience with a man, doesn't mean I can't have a little fun."

"Fun? Yeah, it's all fun and games, Susie. You were gonna sleep with my boss. He's clearly on the rebound. It would be like dating my brother—if I had one." Kate stomped her foot. "It's complicated, admit it. We've had way too much tequila."

"*You* admit the damn problem. You're jealous! He's your type—you can't stand it. He breaks all your good-girl rules, but you don't want *me* to have him. One, he's been married. Two, oh, whatever two is." Susie slurred a bit. "Break your rules about dating a boss—or leave him to me."

"You might be right. It doesn't make me bloody happy."

"Oh, shut up, Kate. I'm leaving in the morning. Do the damn training with him sitting in your classroom, have him all to yourself." Susie, the life-sized Barbie doll, flopped face first on the bed and passed out.

Kate couldn't sleep and checked to see if it was safe to go for a run. *Don't be silly. I love to run at night.* Kate was afraid to go outside—afraid O'Dell would follow her on the trail. She wrote in her journal, scratched out a poem, wadded it up, and threw it in the trash. She finally laid her head on the desk and fell asleep.

When the alarm blared, Susie was gone.

৵ ৵ ৵

Kate braked as a black cat ran out in front of her state-issued Jeep Wrangler. She had been daydreaming and was a block south of the police station.

Black cat crosses my path. What am I supposed to do again? Kate, the lapsed Catholic, made the sign of the cross.

She drove into the police station parking lot, holstered her weapon, and sidestepped out of her Jeep, then she waved at the camera and punched in the code which allowed her access to the back room. She stopped at the dispatcher's window. "Davis working?"

The dispatcher dressed in a blue uniform and studying a report, didn't bother to look up. "Yeah, yeah, he's in the back drinking coffee."

Ron Davis was Kate's friend from high school. He was a few years older and seemed to always be a friend of one of the guys Kate dated. She wanted a brother-sister relationship, but there were whispers Ron wanted it to be more.

Kate walked back to the break room and grabbed a cup of coffee, depositing her quarter into the coffee fund. Davis was sitting at the picnic table in the break room. The table, procured from the park years ago, had initials carved in the wooden top, the work of bored officers over time.

She sat down across from Davis. "Hey, Sarge, how's things going?"

He looked up and grinned. "Hey kid, glad you're back. You wanna ride along tonight?"

"Sure, have to take my stuff home first. How 'bout swinging by later to pick me up? Go for a bite somewhere. My treat."

Davis stood up. "No need for that."

"I'm on expense account, and it's a BOGO night at the Sub Shop."

"Then, dinner's on you. I'll pick you up in a few. I've gotta sign a report."

ᰄ   ᰄ   ᰄ

Kate pulled into her driveway. She touched her gun, holstered on her waist. The weight made it hard for her to exit the Jeep. *I'm gonna need a hip replacement someday.* She smiled to herself, wrestled her suitcase out of the trunk, and dragged it up the one step onto her new porch. She struggled with the new storm door as the north wind blew. She stuck her key into the lock, then pivoted, grabbed her gun, and pointed it low. The suitcase slipped from her fingers and toppled down the steps.

Lights from Davis's patrol car lit up the space. He exited his vehicle, hand on his duty weapon. "What's going on, kiddo?"

"I don't know, Ron." Kate exhaled. She hadn't noticed she'd been holding her breath. "Glad to see you."

Davis double-checked their surroundings and approached the house, then holstered his weapon, and relaxed. He removed his flashlight from his belt, shined the light side to side and moved closer to Kate. "I see a large man's footprint here. Did you spot it in the dark when you approached?"

"No, but there's something about the lock."

"Holster your weapon, I think he's gone. Let's get in the house, park your stuff and we'll have a chat." He picked up her suitcase.

"Okay, thanks. Boy am I glad you're working tonight. I might be paranoid from gun training."

"Yeah, that crap can give you PTSD, but that's not what this is—your instincts are good. He's been here, and unfortunately I know when—me and my big mouth." Ron threw the spotlight on the lock. "Yep, it's been jimmied, he's been inside."

Kate fumbled, but managed to unlock the door. She turned on the kitchen light and gazed around the room.

"Cut the light and grab your flashlight. Keep your voice down." Ron put a finger to his lips.

Kate obeyed and reached into a drawer and found her Maglite. "Why?"

"Shh." He sliced his finger across his throat—the universal language—shut it.

"You think he's listening, don't you?" She looked around the kitchen, searching for any signs of an intruder. Ron handed her a pair of nitrile gloves. Kate slid them on, shaking her head. *I can't believe this is happening*.

They checked the kitchen, living room, bathroom, and finally the bedroom. Kate froze when her beam shone on a Clark candy bar wrapper on the floor to the

30

bedroom. Her stomach turned at the sight of her open lingerie drawer, with her panties and bras pulled from inside and scattered on the dresser and floor.

Ron tucked the wrapper inside an evidence bag. "I'd guess the bastard spent a little time in your lingerie drawer—and he wanted you to know it."

Kate gasped. "Holy crap. I'm burning everything."

The sergeant whispered in the darkness, "You want to report this? I'll run this wrapper, but we might as well face it, he didn't leave any prints."

"What good will it do? I know how this works. He's a cop, the sheriff's cousin. It'll just make me look weak and stupid."

"C'mon, let's go grab a bite to eat and we'll talk. You got somewhere else you can sleep tonight?"

Tears welled in Kate's eyes. "I'll not let him move me from my home. I've lost my appetite."

Davis leaned closer to Kate and whispered, "Well, okay—but we've got to make a plan. You got an attic in this bungalow?"

Kate walked into the hallway and pulled a rope which unfolded a retracting ladder.

"Can you sleep up there tonight? It would be harder for him to get to you without you hearing him."

O'Dell pulled into his parking place a block from Kate's house. He laughed as he swigged on his beer and listened to the two in the house.

This is more fun than deer hunting. That damn fat cop.
He strained to hear as he sat with the amplifier near his ear. *This is going to be so much fun.*

CHAPTER FIVE

CIRCUIT COURT

Matthews sat at Kate's desk in the historic courthouse. Dressed in a black suit, white shirt and blue tie, he lounged in the chair as if he owned the place. "Good Morning Sunshine." He grinned and sat up as Kate walked through the door. *Wow, she cleans up real nice. She looks like a young Sandra Bullock.*

Kate, dressed in a new black suit, short fitted jacket, silk white shirt tucked into a wide waistband, wore tall black leather riding boots. "Mornin', Boss. I've got court in five, I can't be late." She avoided eye contact. "If you'd move, I could pull my files for the docket."

"Of course, sorry—I heard the Judge threw a lawyer in jail last week for being late." Matthews stood up and moved around the desk out of her way.

"Damn straight—and he threatened to throw me in jail because he didn't like my recommendation. So, if you'll excuse me—unless you'd like to take my docket today." Kate looked him in the eye, challenging him.

"No thanks, I'll observe." He stood back, folded his arms, and watched every move she made.

"Great. Like, I need a large man observing me. Judge won't like it." Kate referred to her docket and pulled two more files, placing forms from the files in her briefcase. She studied the array of pens in her drawer and fingered them lightly. She picked three and slotted them in their place. She slammed the briefcase shut and walked out the door, ignoring Matthews.

He followed her up the steps, studying her gait and her ass.

Kate stopped at the top of the second flight of stairs and turned to him. "Stop looking at my ass." She turned back and sprinted up the last flight.

અ અ અ

"All rise! The Circuit Court of Chariton County is now in session, the Honorable Clifford Baxley presiding."

Kate stopped her stride down the aisle and waited for the judge to be seated. She tiptoed a few steps to her seat in the front row of the gallery. Matthews was delayed by the U.S. Marshal who was posted at the door. She smiled. *I hope you don't think you're gonna walk down that aisle and sit next to me after the judge has seated himself.*

She heard the door and the footsteps, but Matthews had seated himself in the back of the courtroom.

Three of Kate's current clients were present, tidy in button-down shirts and dark pants. They sat up straight with freshly cut hair combed in place. When called on by the judge, each responded with "Yes, sir." They were bound over to the next month's court docket—lucky enough to make bail and lucky enough to be coached by Kate Anderson.

Five new arraignments, all in orange jumpsuits—guests of the Chariton County Jail—stood at the same time and remained standing until the last case was heard. They were chained together by one large chain that hung heavy on each handcuffed wrist. One by one, the charges were heard. All five were ordered to be interviewed by Kate before pre-trial. The judge ordered a five-minute recess, and Kate walked over to her new clients.

"My name is Kate Anderson. I'll be down to the jail today or tomorrow to see you."

One of the men in orange whistled, "I can't wait, sweetheart." Matthews stood up in the back of the room. Kate stepped closer to the man in orange. He was at least six inches taller than her five foot six. She looked up at him. "Sir, I'll be down to see you one week from today. Every night before you go to bed, think, 'Gee, that nice lady might have seen me today, if I hadn't opened my big mouth.' And, for your information, a week in jail will cost you two hundred and forty dollars—motel rates." She paused for effect. "Do you have anything else disrespectful to say to me?"

The line of men looked down at their feet.

Kate stepped back and addressed the group. "While you're waiting for me, call your family and tell them you need a place to stay and a job. A job I can verify. Home and a job, that's your ticket out of jail."

She addressed the deputy. "Thanks for waiting. I'll be down as soon as I get a chance." Kate hurried down the aisle, past Matthews, past the U.S. Marshal and into the Ladies Room. On her way out, she took a few seconds to apply some lipstick. She retraced her steps and sat down just in time for the bailiff to call, "All rise."

The next man on the docket was a change of venue from Livingston County. He stood before the judge, represented by his attorney. The formal charge of assault was read, and he waived his right to a preliminary hearing. The client was middle-aged and dressed in a long-sleeved shirt, probably hiding his many tats. The judge stared at him.

"Sir, you are lucky I did not arraign you. Your bail would have been double this amount. I'm placing you on bond supervision. See Miss Anderson before you leave."

Kate got up and walked out of the courtroom with her paperwork. She walked past Matthews, and Benny, the U.S. Marshal, opened the door for her. She addressed the new client. "My name is Kate Anderson and I am your bond investigator. We have a great deal of paperwork to go through, but as you can see, I'm busy with court. Don't leave this courthouse until I see you again, understand?"

The attorney said, "Kate, this man needs to get to work."

"Well counselor, he won't go to work if he gets thrown in jail, will he? I'll get with him when the judge calls a break." She handed her client the paperwork. "Fill it out completely."

Kate returned to the courtroom, received two more clients, and the process was the same. The judge took a fifteen-minute break.

The three clients sat in the foyer waiting, paperwork in hand. Matthews exited the courtroom, walked over to the clients and introduced himself.

Kate approached and said, "Boss, I only have a few minutes to get this done. You've observed enough, haven't you? Can't you see I've got a full day?"

"I'll interview them, it's paperwork." Kate hesitated, but Reese continued. "It's not rocket science, Kate. It's babysitting. You need to know where they are, where they work. I have their appointments scheduled. Go on back to the courtroom—take a breath. You've been running around here like you're killin' chickens or something."

Kate turned and walked back to the courtroom. *Why can't he just leave me alone?*

When Matthews returned to the courtroom, Kate stood and addressed the judge. "Your honor, I beg your pardon sir, but under Missouri Guidelines, I will need supervisor approval before I accept this client."

Kate turned slightly to see if Matthews was in the back of the courtroom. He nodded at her.

"Miss Anderson. Is your supervisor in this courtroom?"

"Yes, Your Honor."

"Both of you approach the bench immediately."

Kate hurried up to the bench. Matthews sauntered down the long aisle from the back of the courtroom.

"Miss Anderson, is it my understanding you brought your boss to work, and you did not see fit to make introductions?"

"No sir—well yes, sir."

Matthews addressed the Judge. "I apologize, Your Honor. Miss Anderson had no idea I would be here today."

"Introduce yourself."

"Reese Matthews, sir—"

"Leave this courtroom immediately and see my assistant. Get the first available appointment. You will not be in this courtroom, observing, without a proper introduction. This woman has a very important job to do and I won't have you distracting her."

"Sir, I'm new here and her job description is a unique one—"

Kate stepped on Reese's toe and looked up at him. *Please shut up.*

"Would you like to see the inside of a cell this morning? Did your investigator bring enough cash with her to bail you both out?"

"No sir, I'll leave. Thank you—sir." Reese started to turn, but Kate stepped on his big toe and pressed down. She whispered up at him. "Your Honor, thank you—Your Honor."

"Your Honor," Reese said.

Kate did not move, she pressed down harder on his toe. He stood still.

"You're dismissed, then." The judge glared down from the bench.

Kate released Reese's toe and turned to stand in her designated spot. "Miss Anderson, you will accept this client. If your administration has a problem with me, they can send someone from the Capital to stand before me."

"Thank you, Your Honor."

CHAPTER SIX

THE OFFICE

T he Parole Office, located in Kingseat's historic district, housed nine parole officers, one clerk, and an investigator who rarely made an appearance. Kate had been assigned to this office six months ago, and had only attended one staff meeting. She turned in her monthly reports by a courier who travelled back and forth between the courthouse and the office twice a week.

Kate knocked on Matthews' door. "You wanted to see me, sir?"

Matthews motioned her in. "Come in, Kate. Have a seat."

"Yes, sir." Kate sat in the office chair next to a pile of boxes. "I see you're moved in."

"You've got quite a job, Ms. Anderson. You keep pretty busy. Who's your backup?"

"No one, sir. I do it myself."

"Wixley didn't have anyone learn your position?" Matthews took a sip of his coffee and looked over the brim at Kate.

"No, sir."

"We could probably dispense with the 'sir.' Do you want a cup of coffee?"

"I don't really have time, inmates in jail, you know. What would you like for me to call you?"

"I can't tell if you're putting me on. After all, you secured me to the floor with your foot yesterday. My big toe is killing me, by the way."

Kate sat up straighter, scooted to the front of her chair, and said, "In case you didn't notice, we—you— were about to get yourself thrown in jail. I've only got bail money for me. I'm old school, taught by nuns— "sir" or "boss." *You* pick it. Besides, you started it with 'Miss Anderson.' What was *that* all about?"

"I think I'll take, 'boss.' 'Sir' sounds like my father."

"Well, you *are* over thirty." Kate grinned and relaxed in her chair.

Matthews grinned, too. "The reason I asked you to come—I've got an appointment to see the judge. I have a hint of what protocol should be with him, but can you give me any pointers?"

"Just be yourself." Kate laughed. "I don't know. He's unpredictable. Like everyone else, he doesn't like change. Wixley stayed away from him. You have another officer who deals with his probationers. You might ask her. But, one point, my clients are not probationers or parolees, they are pretrial clients. It's a thing with him, so don't get it mixed up. And, he wants to be called 'Your Honor.'"

"Why don't you two work together?"

"Why don't you ask her?" Kate could feel herself flush. "She's the senior officer stationed out of this

41

office. I've put in two and half years—six months on *this* job. I don't even have an office here—mine's in the courthouse. I do my work, I get along with the judge, and I attend as many training sessions as I can."

"You two don't get along?"

"We're not cozy friends—never thought about working together, never talked about it—not paid to see the big picture or make your job easier." Kate stood up. "Besides, I think my pay comes from a federal grant. I'm not sure you can mix the money."

"Have a seat, Kate. Tell me about the training sessions you're conducting now."

Kate sat back down on the edge of her seat. "I conduct the *Verbal Judo* segment, you know—the one you partially attended. You'll be getting your grade of "incomplete" in your email. I'm a sub with *Defensive Tactics*. If you think you're gonna cut me, the agency sent me to *Train the Trainer* in Florida. I think I've been assigned."

"How did you get the training assignment?"

"The judge, of course. I slipped him a brochure through his assistant. It was his idea." Kate smiled. "Oh, his assistant likes chocolate. Don't eat her candy. She'll offer you a piece, but don't eat it. Your job is to bring *her* candy. Hershey's Kisses or little chocolate bars."

"Thanks for the tip. You're not getting cut from training. You're being assigned *more* training duties. You've also been tapped as a firearms instructor."

"Firearms instructor? I don't really like guns. I know, I'm a good shot and I went to that advanced training, but it was just to see if I could do it. Training parole officers who have never held a gun? Do you hate me? It's dangerous to be on the range with some of those officers—and I'm not talking about the women."

"Schedule some range time with the police department. You can check out your ammunition today." Matthews stood up and pulled a file from his file cabinet. "You received an excellent review from Wixley. You're taking a class for your master's degree. Continuing education is always a good thing." He looked at Kate who was rearranging his pens. "My only concern with you is—I think the judge may be abusing his authority. A few of these investigations aren't within the scope of your job description."

"No shit." Kate's eyes got big, and she slapped her mouth with the palm of her hand. "Sorry about that, Boss, just kinda slipped out. I wouldn't lead your meeting with the judge with– 'Geez, Judge, I think you're abusing your authority.'" Kate smiled again and relaxed.

"Where's your weapon?" Reese sat back down.

"Locked up at home. I was headed to the jail."

"It's not going to do you any good there is it, Boot?"

"Don't call me 'Boot.'"

"Strap on your gun, and you'll get my respect." He handed Kate a form. "This is a training session I've scheduled for you. It's with the KCPD at the police station in Kansas City. It's called *Street Survival*—it's tomorrow. I assume you know the area?"

"My old stomping ground. Will I be home by six o'clock?"

"Probably not."

"Sounds like three square meals on the State of Missouri. Expense account breakfast, lunch and supper—thanks, Boss." Kate stood up to leave. "I better get busy. I have three interviews in the jail this morning and six coming in this afternoon."

"That many? Really?"

"Yes, really. We're a regional jail. I've also got traveling time to three counties for court dates and Law Days."

"I didn't realize that."

"No, and you scheduled those three appointments yesterday when I'm to be in court in Linn County. So, I'll have to track them down and reschedule. And I see clients in the courthouse, not here."

"I was trying to help. Give me their files and I'll see them. You really going to make that prisoner wait a week for an interview?"

"Maybe. You like being whistled at? Look, I've earned my reputation in the last six months. A little timeout for one guy helps cut down on nonsense. Someone probably dared him to do it. He'll be last, that's for sure. The three clients—thanks, I'll take care of it. I'm used to working alone. I like working alone. Besides, their files are at the courthouse.

"I guess I'm dismissed?"

"Yes, sure—Kate, how much bond money do I need to keep on me?"

"I dunno. I keep three thousand bucks, but the judge likes me. Don't piss him off."

"Again, I don't know if you're putting me on."

"He likes to threaten to throw people in jail. Probably not from an office visit—unless you're late or you're just an ass. Ask your senior staff, visit with Bennie, the Marshal at the courthouse. He's your best source. I understand he also fronts cash for fools. I really need to go, once someone's arrested, I only have forty-eight hours to get them interviewed—unless they piss me off. Just so you know, missing tomorrow will throw me into two late nights. I'll have OT this week."

"Do what you need to do. Your salary's not much— where'd you get three thousand bucks?"

"'Be Prepared'—Girl Scout motto. I've really gotta run. I need to catch the inmates before chow time."

"One more thing, Kate. Why the U.S. Marshal at the courthouse?"

"Am I your only source of info? Geez . . . the judge has had multiple death threats. One credible one. He also carries a very large pistol—like an old gunslinger. Ask to see it."

Kate left the room and then spun around, rapping softly on the doorjamb. "Uh, Boss, could we switch cars tomorrow? Mine's almost due for an oil change and my schedule is jammed. I'll take care of it, day after tomorrow."

"Does yours have gas?" Matthews frowned.

"Always a full tank, Boss."

He opened his desk drawer and threw Kate his keys. She caught them easily with one hand, walked over, and placed her keys on his desk, then turned and quickly strode out the door. "I'll fill out the paperwork on the way out—and ammo, I'll check out ammo. Thanks, Boss!"

CHAPTER SEVEN

THE UNDERGROUND NETWORK

K ate opened the door to Dirty Sally's tavern and let her eyes adjust to the light. The historic bar had flooded several times and survived a fire. It was built before the Civil War from logs pulled from the bottom of the river, logs which were originally cut for fuel to power steamboats.

Kate ordered a whiskey and waved at the huge moose head which hung weary over the bottles of booze. At the base of the huge antler, a small camera was hidden. If Sally, the owner, was in the bar, she would signal from the side door. At age eighty, Sally sashayed like a saloon girl and ran the place with a tight grip on the cash register.

Kate couldn't go home—she didn't want to think about her stalker. As a child, when she wasn't in school, church or fishing, she and Pops visited the bar and played shuffleboard. Sally was one of the few people who had known her father and mother before they were killed in the plane crash.

"Kate, come here." Sally motioned from the side room. Kate picked up her drink, jumped from the barstool, and crossed the tavern, where she hugged the older woman.

"You look beautiful even in your jeans and cowboy boots." Sally leaned in and whispered in Kate's ear. "I've heard you've had some problems."

"You hear everything, don't you, Sally?" Kate peered over the owner's shoulder and stared into the darkness of the inner room.

Sally stepped back and wagged her finger at Kate. "It's been months since I've seen you. You've never been in the back room, have you?"

"No, Sally, I haven't been in your secret room—you know that." Kate walked into the private area. A pentagon-shaped bar was set in the middle, with poker tables arranged a couple of feet from each of the five corners, allowing easy access for waitresses to serve drinks, while preventing players from spying on other games. Booths lined the back wall, and a waitress in a short seventies-style mini skirt delivered a heaping bowl of beef stew to a table. Kate followed her nose and saw a woman in a back booth who looked like a "Rosie the Riveter" poster.

"No poker games tonight?" asked Kate.

"Saturday nights and a few special events fund a particular project of mine. The rest of the time, invited guests only," said Sally.

Sally followed Kate's gaze. "Let's go meet Rosie."

Kate walked behind Sally over to the booth. The older woman sat down gracefully, slipping easily across the seat. Kate pulled a chair up to the end of the booth.

"Rosie, this is Kate Anderson. Give her one of your business cards."

"Yes, ma'am." Rosie pulled a rumpled business card from the pocket of her man's shirt.

"She might need a transport at some time in the near future."

"I will?" Kate studied the card, which read *Rosie Martin, Trucker.*

"It's all good, Sally. I've known Kate since she was a little girl." Rosie turned towards Kate. "Your grandfather helped me when no one else would. My husband threw me and my kid out into the street. My parents wouldn't take me in. Your grandfather gave me a paycheck up front, fed me, and gave me a job. Saved me from having to crawl back to that dick of a husband of mine—or any other dick for that matter."

"*My* grandfather?"

"Yeah, Theodore Anderson." Rosie laughed. "I worked as clean-up and laundry lady, stayed in the back room of the T & H Wholesale store. I laundered the t-shirts, swept the warehouse, stocked shelves, set traps for mice. One day, a driver called in sick and your granddad was planning to take the route himself. I told him, 'I can drive a truck.'

"He took me out to the parking lot and told me to back the truck up to the loading dock. No problem." Rosie shook her head. "Ted laughed and said he could do lots of things, but backing a truck was not one of them. He gave me a driver's job and a man's wages—unheard of in that day."

"Thanks for telling me. I don't often hear nice stories about Pops." Kate slid the business card into the back pocket of her Levis.

"Don't lose that." Sally wagged her finger at Kate.

"I won't. I don't know why I'll need it, but I'll put it in my card file."

Sally stood up. "Excuse us, Rosie, but as you know—I have a lot of work to do."

"You always do." Rosie turned her attention to her beef stew and homemade bread.

"Let's go in the kitchen, honey."

Kate followed Sally into the kitchen.

"You remember Sister Anne?"

"Sister, what are *you* doing here?"

"God's work." Sister Anne embraced Kate.

"You look wonderful, Sister, not a day older than when I last saw you."

Sally interrupted the two women. "Kate will be volunteering in the kitchen two nights a week. She needs to learn how to make pies and bread."

"What? I feel like *Alice in Wonderland* and I just fell down the rabbit hole," Kate said.

"You did, but you are one of the lucky ones. Kate, you need skills—skills you didn't learn at home. Not that your Grandma Helen or your Amish nanny couldn't have taught them to you. Face it—what would happen to you if you couldn't do the job you have now?"

"I'd go to law school. I'm taking intro classes, but please don't tell Pops."

"Kate, what if that wasn't an option? What if you had to go on the run?"

Kate walked out of the kitchen, the steel doors swinging as she pushed through them and left the room. She scooted into the booth across from Rosie.

"What's going on here? I've known since I was a kid that Sally dealt in the underground, the world ordinary people rarely see, but what *is* this really? Level with me. I have your card—you must be my sponsor or something."

Rosie stared at Kate. "Sally's been involved in an underground network for forty-some years now. She's organized a group across the country to move abused women to a new life. Some would lose their lives without Sally. They follow much the same path as slaves took before Lincoln freed them, heading for Canada, the land of the free."

"What does it have to do with me?"

"You need to wake up, girl!" Rosie banged her fist on the table. "You've got a real bad man marking you as his. He's an animal. He's in a relationship with you— no doubt taking pictures, pretending you are his wife or his girlfriend, or worse yet, prey. He's not gonna stop until you're dead or worse—sold. He's playing with his catch, he's stalking you, staking out his territory— peeing on trees. When the time comes, and it *will* come—you get your ass to Sally's, the convent, or call that number. You hear me? You may have weeks, or months, but pack your bag, get your affairs in order."

"I can't run, I've got a life here."

Rosie's face hardened. "You think any woman who's abused doesn't have a life? They've got a life. Like I said, girl—you need to wake up. If you don't—you're gonna find yourself in a very ugly place. That would break that old lady's heart."

Kate sat staring at Rosie. She put her head in her hands and shook her head. "How did this happen?"

Rosie moved toward the end of the booth, placed one hand on her leg and the other on the side of the table before she hoisted herself up. "I'm crippled because of a man. Don't let it happen to you. I gotta go, miles to go before I rest. Anyway, here comes Sally. I think she has a present for you."

Kate turned and managed a weak smile. "A present for *me*?"

"Yes, dear girl, a present." She pointed to the back door of the building. As they exited, Kate heard puppies barking. A young man with a dark face, dressed in a black-hooded sweatshirt, approached, holding a very wiggly puppy.

Kate looked at the young man who she could barely see and realized he was not African American but that he had darkened his face. Confusion met joy when he held the puppy out to her.

"For me? My goodness. Hello, sweetheart. Aren't you beautiful? Sally, a puppy, you're giving me a puppy?" She held the dog close to her. "What's his name?"

"Sic'em," Sally said.

"Sic'em is his name?" Kate laughed. "Hello Sic'em. We might have to change your name." She kissed the puppy's head.

Sally pointed at the pup. "He's a full-blooded German Shepherd and comes from a powerful line. He will make a wonderful guard dog and companion for you, Kate. But you can't take him tonight. He's not been weaned, and he has more training with Dennis. Dennis is teaching him basic commands and will also do the potty training. When you come this week to volunteer in the kitchen, you can see Sic'em and walk him. You will be trained in commands."

"How will I repay you? I just paid for my duty weapon, and I guess I also need a backup weapon. I'm a little strapped for cash."

"I plan to put you to work, Kate. Nothing in life is free."

Kate looked at the wriggly puppy as it licked her face and attempted to bark. "Oh, you're so cute—someday you will bark like a big dog." She kissed the dog's head and returned him to Dennis. "Thank you, Dennis."

Kate hugged Sally. "I'm going to listen carefully and do whatever you say. I know I'm in trouble and I've been really scared. You've given me hope."

Sally smiled. "I bet you're hungry. We have beef stew and homemade bread."

"That sounds good. You're not gonna make me do anything illegal, are you? I mean, this isn't Mafia Godmother is it?" Kate grinned.

"We'll see, Kate." Sally threw her arm around Kate and they returned to the bar.

CHAPTER EIGHT

STREET SURVIVAL

K ate swore under her breath as she circled the courthouse looking for a parking space. Damn. I'm going to be late. She looked at her watch, swore again, and pulled into a paid parking lot. She could not be late for street survival training.

Jumping out of her car, she smiled at the grimy attendant. "That car better be here when I get back—I'll bring you a donut."

"Yeah, yeah. Take your ticket," the parking attendant muttered, never looking up.

Kate ran across the midsection of the street, dodging cars stopped at the red light. She entered the building and sprinted up a flight of stairs to the training room. After grabbing a cup of coffee in a small Styrofoam cup, she tried to find an end seat for a quick exit. All good cops used that trick. She spotted a seat in the third row, stuck in the middle of Kansas City cops, mostly men.

Once seated, Kate turned to her left, "Hi, my name is Kate."

Before the man could answer, the lights went out and the room turned to pitch-black. Kate leaned down and placed her coffee on the floor.

A loud voice came over the speaker, "How fast can you die?" Boom! A gunshot echoed in the room. The noise was deafening. Kate slid to the floor, crouching like a scared rabbit when a second shot blasted.

Holy shit. Sounded like a shotgun. What the hell is going on? She slid further down on the floor between seats, her arms wrapped around her knees. An officer with a flashlight stepped over her as she placed her hands over her head, and then three more stepped over her.

The lights came on; an officer reached down and helped her up. His very white teeth were the only thing Kate could see as her eyes adjusted.

"You weren't prepared for the blast, were you?"

"Nope. Thanks for the lift up." Kate stood, brushing off her butt.

"Your boss is an ass." The man's eyes crinkled as he grinned at her.

Kate's heart pounded from the adrenaline surge. "Yeah." She looked for her coffee which had puddled underneath the seat in front of her.

"Just leave it; they'll get it later." He put out his hand. "I'm Pete Marlow. I'm a technician for KCPD. Most everyone is prepared for the shots, except a few. You're not from here?"

"Kate Anderson—"

A man dressed in Kansas City police riot gear took the stage. "What did we learn, men?"

The audience reseated themselves and sat straight in their chairs.

"I'll tell you what you learned—there are 'reactors' and there are 'freezers.' I don't care if you tried to pull your weapon; I don't care if you dove under the seat. This is all I care about: when I fired that weapon, no one was sitting frozen in their chair. I would have reported any 'freezers' to their supervisor and excused them from the rest of the class." The instructor paused. He was looking straight at Kate. She stared back at him.

"Now, we're going to watch some shoot/don't shoot videos. We're acclimating you into these scenarios, so no one gets PTSD. If you're in this class, there's a reason you're here. Has your boss chosen you to take this class because you're weak? Has he tapped you as a 'freezer?'" The man amped his voice louder. "You better not be a 'freezer!' If you're a 'freezer'—do everybody a big favor and find a new line of work."

Kate scowled. *Reese Matthews, you're an ass. I wonder if you know about my stalker?*

৵   ৵   ৵

Kate met Susie Jones for lunch in a dive diner close to the training center. She wound her way through the small, crowded space, and found Susie waiting at a table with two plates of ribs, coleslaw, hush puppies, home fries, and sweet tea. She leaned down and hugged her friend, who was chewing on a rib. "Nice spread. Thanks so much for meeting me, Susie. I'm really sorry about our fight."

"Me too, and I hate to admit it, but you were right. Tequila is not our friend. We're not kids anymore."

"Has Matthews called you?"

"He's texted me. I've played him a bit to see if I could get info from him, but he holds his cards pretty close to his chest."

"Everything's a test with him. He's meeting the judge today." Kate grinned. "I secretly hope he's thrown in jail." She took a long drink of the iced tea. "He assigned me to this 'Street Survival' training and everyone in the room knew this A-hole trainer was going to fire a weapon at the beginning of class—everyone except for me. Ninety-something men, five or so women. Just threw me into it, no warning. It was two shotgun blasts."

Susie finished her rib. "Shit! He *is* an A-hole. But he knew you could handle it. I would forgive him for his sins." She smiled at Kate.

Kate laughed. "I get it, Susie. You've got the hots for him. I'm telling you, it's not easy for me. He smells great." Kate sniffed the air. "All the female officers are goo-goo-eyed over him. I guess they're all too stupid to know they can kiss their career goodbye if they sleep with the boss."

"I wouldn't care," Susie giggled. "But, then again, I'm a short-timer. Eat, Kate."

"I'm trying to just stay away from him. Hey, you want to skip out this afternoon? I've checked my training itinerary—same boring stuff."

"You better go back, and besides—I'm doing some off-book work for a private investigator. His name is Pete Marlow."

"Get outta here. I just met him. He pulled me off the floor after the shots were fired. You're working for him?" Kate lowered her voice. "You can't do that without supervisor approval."

"You crack me up, Kate. The rules you keep—the rules you break. Look, we're not long-term state employees. We've got to have a 'plan B' and it might as well start now. There's better money in the private sector and technology is where it's at. After your close call in the jail, I realized it's not my scene. I've got to get out. Behind a computer screen is where I want to be."

Susie shoved a file over to Kate. "Marlow dug up some info on your unwelcome boyfriend. This guy's hard core, Kate. He's *really* connected." Susie counted, licking her barbecued fingers one by one: "He's your sheriff's cousin. He's got U.S. marshals as basketball buddies. He's in a biker gang." Susie's blue eyes widened. "You're not holding out on me, are you, Kate? You only dated him once?"

"However you count it. I met him when I lived here in KC—about seven months ago in the Jazz Bar. We had a great conversation and had so much in common. We knew the same people, same places—it seemed like a great fit. He was charming and sent me roses, but I was headed to south Missouri for that gun training. Then he showed up. It seemed too much of a coincidence, and it felt creepy. No doubt he stalked me there."

"I'm asking because this PI thinks it might make a difference. There are different types of stalkers, those who can't let their wives or girlfriends go— and then guys who prey on women."

"Yeah, I'm getting the same feedback."

Susie looked at Kate. "What do you mean?"

"Oh, another long story. I'll tell you soon. I better get back. Are you sure you can't skip out?" Kate gave Susie a persuasive grin, "C'mon, we'll go see a foreign film."

"I can't. I'm trying to complete my assignments with Marlow on time. Go back to your training session. Talk to him if you can."

"The rules you keep—the rules you break, Susie."

"We're a lot alike, Kate."

"Okay, I've got to tell you one more thing before we go. I'm getting a dog. His name is Sic'em. He's the cutest German Shepherd puppy you will ever see. He's already fierce, and he'll bark like a big dog."

"A *dog*? A damn *dog*? A slobbery *mess* of a dog? Sic'em—that's the stupidest name I've ever heard."

"I know, isn't it great?"

"Yeah, great. A slobbery, hairy dog—one you have to go home and feed and let out. Why don't you just have a baby? I know, a baby with Reese Matthews."

"Oh, shut up, Susie. You're gonna love him—the dog. Just wait and see."

Susie finished her tea. "No dogs allowed at my house. You better find a great pet sitter. I mean it—no slobby, hairy dog at *my* house."

"Susie, thanks for the file on O'Dell, but I don't want to know anything about him."

"No, Kate. Listen to me. It's time for you to investigate your stalker."

CHAPTER NINE

CAR CHASE

Kate rapped on the wooden gate to the lot behind Dirty Sally's, where Dennis was playing with Sic'em. She opened the gate and emerged into the light, admiring Dennis' handiwork. Park lights circled the space and solar lights accented a path to a rustic cabin, once a shed, now transformed into an energy-efficient home. Dennis had replaced the broken windows, installed new flooring throughout the house, and placed a custom-made bed in the small, closet-sized bedroom. He had also built a deck in front and planted a garden out back, after clearing the entire space with a shovel and a wheelbarrow.

"Sic'em, come!" Kate patted her chest, and the puppy jumped into her arms.

Dennis stood up and approached Kate. "You know that's a really bad habit. That dog is going to be a monster all too soon."

"I know, you've told me, but it's fun. Hello boy, how's my good boy today?" The dog licked Kate's face and whimpered. She set the dog on the ground. "Sit, Sic'em." The dog obeyed, looking up at her.

Kate turned to Dennis, "I've not seen this place lit up. It's really fantastic. You've built a little private compound back here."

"Did you get your pie dough perfected?"

"Finally, thank goodness. Sister Anne is a perfectionist. I didn't think I would ever please her. Will I be taking Sic'em home soon?"

The dog, hearing his name, barked. Kate laughed and snuck him a treat.

"Yes, next week. Don't undo all my training, okay?"

"Does it mean I won't see you anymore?" Kate wrestled with the puppy, pulling on a teething rope.

"No, I've got work to do at your place. Sally said you need a carpenter. What do you have planned? I can start tomorrow."

"That's wonderful. I'll put Sic'em with Momma. I'm running late tonight, sorry, Dennis."

"No problem, I got your text. Sic'em can sit under the kitchen table."

"He can't sit on my lap?"

"No, Kate, he's a guard dog."

Kate leashed the dog, "Sic'em, heel." They walked the path that led to the house. "Did you do all this work yourself?"

"Yeah, this place was a pit when I got here. I was a grateful pup myself, but there was just a sleeping bag on the floor. I made the table, the beds, the cabinets, well everything. Can I get you some lemonade?"

"You got anything stronger? I've had a long day driving to the city and back."

"Nah, not in this house. You're welcome to go back to the bar and grab something."

"Oh, no problem. Lemonade sounds delicious."

Dennis filled two glasses with ice and lemonade and gave one to Kate. They settled at the kitchen table. "Tell me about your plans for your house."

"I've got a small attic with a window, and I would like to utilize the space with a bed and some basic shelves. Right now, all I have is a blow-up mattress there. I could use an electrical outlet for a fan and a small reading light. I'd like to be able to get out the window, but for no one to be able to crawl in."

"I get it, you've got a tactical advantage from above, in case you have an intruder. No problem. You can order a "bed-in-a-box," and we should be able to get it through the hole . . . or do you have stairs?"

"It's just a hole. I'd like pull-down stairs. I think the air bed is fine. In the kitchen, I want a small doggie door with a secure lock on the inside. I'm hoping Sic'em can still get through it when he's giant-sized."

"Oh, he'll figure it out."

"And, I know this is a little bizarre, but I want a telescoping peep hole in the front door. I want to look out and extend a telescope to a location about two blocks away."

Dennis scratched his head. "Well, that may take some doing. I don't think you want it to extend out, just look through the hole like it is a telescope. It won't be any good for someone knocking on your door. You won't be able to see them. Or, he might put tape over it or spray it with paint."

Kate shivered. "I hadn't thought of that." She took a drink of her lemonade. "Maybe a peephole and a telescope."

"Hmm, well, let me do some research. I know a guy with gadgets. You've changed your locks?"

"Yes, immediately after the break in. I'm surprised you know about that."

"Small community, we've got to talk about something."

"Everybody's pretty tight-lipped around me. I'm learning to waitress, bake, and I'm brushing up on my Spanish. Nobody tells me anything. Why is Sister Anne here? Never mind, you're not telling me either—I'm inside the community, but I'm outside. Let's change the subject. Dennis, where did you learn to train dogs?"

"In prison."

Kate stared at him. "Do you have false eyelashes on? And—your face—it's a different color from the other night."

Dennis chuckled and reached up and touched his eyes. "I forgot. I can't tell you anything. Let's get back to the job. I learned my carpentry skills at vo-tech school while in high school. I'll do a good job for you. I make fifteen dollars an hour and I'll need cash for some supplies. When I figure out something on your spy gear, that'll be more."

"Sure—no problem." Kate stood up.

"I'll be there tomorrow morning about seven. Can you meet me at lunch and lock up?"

"I can just give you the key."

"No—never do that again, " Dennis said.

"How stupid of me—"

"You can't trust anyone."

Kate looked at the man and studied his features. "Dennis O'Malley's not your real name, is it?"

"The less you know the better. But no."

"So, this boot camp Sally has me in, does it involve a class in make-up? What disguise will you wear to my house tomorrow?"

"Do you need a class in make-up? I'll be glad to give you one." Dennis grinned.

"Are you going to be around that long?"

The young man looked down and shuffled his feet. "I hope so, but I don't know."

"I'm sorry. I'm so insensitive. I work with a bunch of jerks, and we tease each other all the time. Do you want to come in the bar and try a piece of my pie? I'm sure it's cooled by now."

"It's okay. I've made a little home here but have learned to have gypsy feet. I hope it doesn't happen to you. No on the pie, they'll save me a piece."

"Suit yourself, but I'm having me a piece of pie right now—I'm starving—and I'm bringing half of it home with me. I'll see you tomorrow, bright and early."

"Kate, here's a package for you from Sally. Take it. Open it as soon as you get home."

⇜ ⇜ ⇜

Kate drove out to the highway, taking a different route home and making sure she was not being followed. It was the long way around, travelling the blacktop roads Z to ZZ to 5. She looked over at her package, a white box with a small piece of duct tape on the side. *I wonder what this is, a box of make-up? Oh, crap, I bet it's a stolen gun.*

She looked in her review mirror and saw headlights. She placed her hand on her revolver which lay ready on the front seat of her boss's Jeep Wrangler and tried to study the headlights, but the vehicle loomed large in her rearview mirror. She felt like her heart might jump out of her chest. *It's a large pickup—and I'm in the middle of nowhere.*

The pickup—a dark-colored Dodge—crossed the yellow line and started to pass her on the unlit, two-lane blacktop. She slowed a little as the vehicle passed her Jeep. She could see the driver. O'Dell grinned at her.

I should just shoot him.

She slammed on her brakes, skidding to a stop, then executed a near-perfect highway-patrol turnaround and accelerated in the opposite direction at a high rate of speed. She drove in a straight line to Matthews' house and searched for his garage door opener, locating it on the visor. She punched the button. The door opened and Kate drove into his garage, braking hard just in time to avoid running into a large cabinet. She punched the button again, and the door began to lower.

Kate jumped out of the vehicle and crouched low, her Smith and Wesson in hand. She looked up to see Matthews standing in the door of his garage, a Glock lowered at his side.

"Don't shoot, lady! I could ask, what the hell are you doing here? But I think I know."

Kate grinned and stood up. "You sounded just like John Wayne. You should have said, 'little lady.' Umm . . . want some pie? Sister Anne makes the best pies."

"Bring it in, I'll make some coffee."

CHAPTER TEN

NIGHT VISIT

Holstering her weapon, Kate retrieved the pie from the floor of the Jeep and peeked inside the container. Looks okay to me. She glanced at the white box, which had slid against the door during her turnaround in the road, left it, and followed Matthews, who was waiting for her to enter the house.

"Watching a Chiefs' game? Don't turn it off because of me," Kate said as Reese switched the large screen TV to mute. She searched for a place to set the pie, but the kitchen table was piled high with work files—*her* files, she noted.

Don't trust anyone. McBride's voice echoed in her head.

Matthews carried the files to the living room table next to the only chair in the room—a large, camouflaged recliner. She set the pie down on the surface of the table and rearranged her belt, heavy with her Smith and Wesson. She studied him. *He looks so much younger dressed in his Chiefs' flannels. I caught him in his jammies.*

"I think I've got a couple of clean plates. Who'd you say made the pie? It's still warm, I can smell it."

"Never mind—don't make me lie to you. You might beat me to it—you look suspiciously like a pie thief." Gone was the rigid edge to her voice now she was not in the office.

"Okay, sounds like a dare, a little investigation of my own. I love cherry pie and late-night visits from beautiful women."

"Do ya now? Well this isn't that kind of visit." Kate glared at him.

He held his hands up. "Don't shoot, little lady, I'm unarmed."

"The hell you are. Where do you have it, ankle holster?"

"Nope . . . but you should go to the pawn shop, there's a nice woman who will find you a backup."

"I think I might have found one, but thanks." *It's probably in your Jeep right now.*

He laid out plates, forks, and paper towels as napkins, and handed her a serrated edge knife. When their hands touched, she hoped he did not feel the electric charge that ran up her arm.

"You do the honors and cut the pie. I've got milk and coffee. I thought you had a pie. Where's the other half?"

"Well it would've been rude to take someone's whole pie now, wouldn't it? I better do milk, if it's not spoiled. I'm jittery enough."

He poured a cup of coffee and a glass of milk. "I just moved in—the milk hasn't had time to sour. You can park your weapon over there next to mine, unless you think you're gonna need it." He grinned and motioned to a small stand next to the back door.

"Thanks." She unholstered her weapon and laid it next to his. "No questions—let's just enjoy our heavenly baked treat."

"Sit down, make yourself at home."

"Okay, thanks." Peeking in on the game, Kate sat at the small round table and looked around the room. The two ate in silence for a minute. Reese spoke first. "This is really good pie, who'd you say made it?" He grinned as he lowered his fork. "You saving that last piece for someone special or you gonna split it with me?"

"I think I'll split it with you. You're not really going to make me be a gun trainer, are you?"

"Firearms instructor. I'm not gonna make you do anything. You thought the department needed a woman trainer and, I think your exact words were, 'women shoot guns differently than men.'" He paused. "You really don't want to do it? Develop your own course designed for women?"

"No, I don't want to do it, but it might be like eating broccoli—it'll be good for me."

"Wise woman."

"Reese, I'm a different person since I've started carrying a gun. I worry all the time that someone will take it away from me and kill someone. I also worry . . . well, uh, I just *reacted* tonight. The training is working, and I'm getting some skills. I was scared, but it didn't seem real. I feel like the department is turning me into a trained killer."

"I understand. It's something every military person or law enforcement officer goes through. You'll have to settle it in your own mind."

"I know." Kate looked out the window. "Susie might be right, it's time for us to get out."

"Kate, you've got great reflexes and good instinct. The department needs strong women, but it may not be for you. We can also put you in a public relations position. You'd be great at that. Think about it."

"I will, thanks." Kate looked out the window again. *I wonder if O'Dell followed me here and is watching from the street.*

"I should tell you, Ron Davis is really sick."

"I know. Cindy, his wife, called. He's a tough old bird. She says she's not worried, but I know she is."

"Do you want to take some time off work? Go down to see him? You have the time. I can arrange to have a bond investigator from the city come in . . ."

"Susie—you've already figured out a way to get her here. You'd be playing with fire, Boss."

"It's 'Boss' now, Kate? And there's a hardness to your voice. We were down-home friendly—you drove into my garage like you owned the place—now you're all business. What's up with that?"

"I honestly don't know. You're just trying to help me. No, I don't want off work. Ron doesn't want me to see him that way. Male pride, I guess. I really grew up after I realized the sacrifices veterans make. He's my first hero. You know he would take a bullet for me."

"I'm sure that's true. If you change your mind, let me know. It would be fun for you to have Susie here."

"So, I guess you wondered why I drove right into your garage. Would you believe me if I said I was testing your skills and wanted to see if you would shoot me?"

"Well, you can try, but I'm on your side. If you have a problem, especially if it involves your work, tell me."

"I'll try to keep it simple. I have a stalker, and he's a deputy related to the sheriff. I got a restraining order. It happened when I was in south Missouri at training. The judge down south issued it to go both ways. It's on my permanent record. But I can't carry a gun with a restraining order, so I had to drop the order. He can't carry a gun with a restraining order, either.

"Is that why you resisted carrying a weapon?"

"Partly, I wanted to keep the restraining order, because he scared me, but what good did the order really do? It's a piece of paper. He'll carry a gun anyway—and it would be worse if he got fired from his job. I won't hang my head about this—it's happened before. I had a stalker in high school. I guess I just attract them."

"Really, what happened in that case?"

"I pressed charges, and the guy went to jail. He came out and started calling me. I went to college—and then he died."

"He died? What?"

"I know, twenty-something-year-old man dies? I was in college, Pops said not to worry about it. I didn't. Now that we're talking about it . . . it's weird, isn't it?"

"I'm telling everyone not to mess with Kate Anderson."

She picked up the plates and put them in the sink, then grabbed a coffee mug and poured herself a cup.

"Robert O'Dell's his name. He's been calling—in the middle of the night, saying nasty things. I thought he was following me tonight. I panicked and drove straight into your garage. I know you've been checking up on me—none of this is news to you."

"Tell me the truth, Kate. Robert O'Dell following you tonight?"

"It *was* Robert, I think. Now I wonder if I might just be paranoid. How did he know *I* was driving *your* car?" Kate smiled. "You think I'd be sharing that pie with you, if I had thought this through?"

"You should've told me."

"I've always kept my personal life out of the office. It's just not . . . professional to do anything else."

"I run my office more like a team. I was in the military. You're on my team, Kate. The team is only as strong as its weakest link. How'd you know where I live?"

She laughed. "This is a small town. Everybody knows where you live. You're the most eligible bachelor in this county. Didn't you read your own newspaper article? Cracked me up. Get ready for widows carrying casseroles."

"How old do you think I am? Surely, not widows?"

"Cougars, Reese. I better go. Do you want to take me to my car? It wasn't out front."

"I had it delivered to your house after I had the oil changed. I guess I'll get to see where you live."

"Oh, never mind, I'll just run home."

Reese stood up. "Stay right there. I'll throw on some jeans. You're *not* running home, Kate."

"Okay, I need to arrange some things in the car. I'll meet you in the garage."

CHAPTER ELEVEN

SHERIFF'S VISIT

T he sheriff sat with his feet up on his desk reading the night's log sheets. He sipped coffee from a cup stamped in big red letters: "#1 Dad." He filled it a little too full, dribbling the coffee onto his brown shirt. "Damn."

Setting his cup down, he looked at the camera showing the view of the street. "Just what I need, that big son-of-a-bitch. What does he want?"

Matthews exited his Jeep and strode over to the front door. The door buzzed open before he pushed the button. He walked into the lobby and barked at the young man behind the bulletproof glass. "Tell Sheriff O'Dell, I'm here."

"Sir, he knows, and said to tell you he's busy."

"Tell him—I've got info he might need." The second door buzzed, and Matthews swung it wide open. He marched down the hall to the sheriff's office.

"What the hell you want, Matthews?"

"Hell of a greeting this morning, Sheriff. Did you wake up on the wrong side of the bed?"

The man behind the desk didn't bother to look up. "State your business, Matthews, I've got work to do."

"What's the deal with your nephew back-handing one of my investigators?"

"Look Matthews, the way I hear it—the way the sheriff's report read, your girl did plenty of her own swinging. Robert had a bloody nose and a very sore groin. And—he's not my nephew—he's a cousin."

"She should have shot him."

"Best you stay out of their business." The sheriff sipped his coffee. "Besides, she should've thought before spending a magical week with a guy she barely knew. I guess she's a little fireball."

"Watch your mouth." Matthews stood up tall.

The sheriff pulled his feet off the desk and sat up straight. "Look Matthews, there's no reason for us to get into this business. This will cool down on its own—don't go buttin' your big nose into it. Ask your good buddy in the governor's office about my cousin. He'll tell you, Robert's a great cop and a valuable asset to his office."

"I'll do just that. I'm sure the governor doesn't want a man on his team that slaps a woman half his size."

The exchange was much like a giant Great Dane barking at a skinny miniature Doberman Pinscher.

"Look, let's just cool down, okay? I think we're on the same side here. Think about it, if Robert loses his job, he'll be here more—and less time he's likely to find a new female interest."

"No—we're not on the same side. Men don't raise their hands to women. They don't sit a half block away and spy on them."

"I'll agree. But there's not much I can do. He's not breaking any laws. She dropped the restraining order—and you're also in the wrong office. This falls on the city cops."

"You know why she dropped the protection order. Law says neither one of them would be able to carry a gun. She would abide by it, he wouldn't—having a sheriff in his pocket."

"Listen here. I'm in nobody's pocket and I'm not in yours—or hers. The prosecutor has a tap on her phone line, trying to get him on a harassment charge. Look Matthews, we're never going to like each other. I catch the bad guys, y'all let them out. You fill my jail with probation violators who should have gone to prison in the first place. Then, you let them out—for me to have to arrest all over again. Revolving damn door you and your kind created."

"You don't like us unless you need us to issue a warrant or conduct a search."

"Isn't that why you're here today?"

"Can't say I didn't try. If Kate shoots the asshole—well—I tried."

"If she shoots the asshole, she'll need more than that three-thousand dollars she's stuffed in her bra to bail herself out. Don't let the door hit you in the ass on the way out."

Matthews scratched his head. "You got any coffee? Maybe it was me who got up on the wrong side of the bed. I saw her last night, and she's scared."

The sheriff pointed to the coffee pot. "Help yourself and pour me some." He handed his cup to Matthews.

"You're like a dog with a bone. You never give up, do you?"

Matthews walked over, picked up the pot, and looked for a clean cup. There were three mugs on the counter. All appeared to be crusted with mold. Matthews found a disposable white cup in the top of a small cupboard.

"You don't like guys drinking your coffee, do you?"

"Nope, damn mooches. Where'd you find that clean cup?"

"Not my first sheriff's office; they're usually stashed somewhere. You know we could find you someone with community service to clean your office." Matthews handed the sheriff his cup.

"Community service workers—lazy idiots—I'd just as soon keep my stuff private."

Matthews looked over at the trash can piled high with papers and candy wrappers.

The sheriff followed his gaze, "Yeah, I could take out the trash. We gonna chaw about trash—or are you gonna leave?"

"Robert O'Dell, he got a history of hitting women?"

"I don't know, he's a cousin—younger than me."

"Sheriff, I know blood's thick, but I've known you since—what, 2001?—when we met at the training in the Lake of the Ozarks. You're a decent family man. I'm appealing to your family pride. I don't want to get on the wrong side of you, but if you don't want to check into this guy—I'm gonna whether you like it or not."

"Okay, okay, I'll level with you. I like Kate, she does a great job. She handles that lunatic judge. The deputies like her—hell, she helps most of them. She stops in, fetches dinner for them, brings 'em treats, fills the dispatcher's coffee so he doesn't have to leave his post. One night, she was tutoring a deputy's son in Spanish. It's hard not to like the girl."

Matthews stared at the man and sat down. "Go on."

"I don't know why she'd get involved with a feller like Robert—I don't know that she did. I guess she's a great natural shot. He's a great shot, but *he's* been trained. The FBI trainers set up a friendly competition between the two of them. I think they were trying to get rid of her, because she's a PO. She might have beat him if she hadn't got trigger finger."

"So, you've been checking up on them?"

"My county—yeah, my job. You really think I didn't care about this? I pulled some strings and got the video tape from the restaurant. The cops down south didn't want to investigate. Cops investigating cops. It was better to sweep it under the rug. That little town depends on the FBI academy for the business it brings in. Robert back-handed her pretty good. She's a fighter."

"Why didn't you just say so?"

"I didn't want you nosing into it. I've got a couple guys checking into some things. Can you just leave it for about a week?"

"You suspect him of doing this before?"

"Surely you understand you can't be in on this—hell, I can't really be in on this. Robert's connected with all sorts of law enforcement and other real badasses.

They're like brothers. I'm also working with the police. Ron Davis is doing a joint investigation with us."

"You investigating—dirty cops?"

"Don't be jumping to any conclusions. Let's just say, we're following several leads—"

"Tell me, damn it," Matthews said.

"Missing women. We're running a task force investigating missing women. Robert's a person of interest. If we let Robert think he's safe, and she's not going anywhere, I think your girl is relatively safe. Davis's keeping a close eye on her."

"You're using her as bait to track his movements and keep him occupied while you investigate?"

"Something like that. I don't care if he's my cousin— he might be a bad seed."

CHAPTER TWELVE

DENISE

K ate pushed the button on her coffeepot and started washing the blue-flowered dishes that spilled out of her sink. *How can these dishes pile up like this? I'm rarely home.* She watched out the window for Dennis, then stiffened as she heard a knock followed by a hard rattle as someone shook the knob on her front door. She jumped and ran to it. *No one ever comes to the front door, surely Dennis would know to come to the back of the house.* With her hand on the deadbolt, she said, "Who is it?"

"Your carpenter."

"Dennis, is that you?"

"Yeah, open the door."

Kate opened the door to a woman dressed in a pink tank top, her perky breasts standing up in the morning air. Her spiked hair looked like she had raked it with a meat fork. She carried a beat-up silver toolbox and her tool belt hung low around her small waist.

"Good morning, Miss Kate." She laughed a high-pitched donkey laugh, ending with a little snort.

J.J. Clarke

"Dennis? Wow, you look—different."

"You can call me Denise. Just Denise."

"So that explains the sparkly make-up from the other night. I thought you were in a drag show or something. Why are you Dennis at the bar, isn't the bar safe?"

Another high-pitched laugh. "Are you going to let me in or what?"

Denise stepped into the house and placed her toolbox on the floor. "No questions, Kate. First, is this the door? The one where you want the telescoping peep hole? Show me around, I'm sure you don't have much time before you need to leave for work. I drove by that creep's parking place today. It's beside the football field, right?"

"Yes, that's where he parks, sometimes. He's now on this kick to follow me."

"I'm going to leave him a little present—some nails and screws. Maybe we can give him a big flat tire or a blow-out."

"I didn't hear that. You want a cup of coffee?"

"You're kinda a goody two-shoes, aren't you? Don't play southern hospitality with me, I'll help myself. The door's good and solid, lock's good. Of course, he's a sheriff's deputy so he could ram it."

"My friend Ron's been here and made a threat assessment. That's why I'm sleeping in the attic."

"Show me."

The two women walked through the living room into the hallway. "Up there is my little make-shift bedroom."

82

Denise climbed the ladder, peeked into the space, and disappeared. In a few minutes, she put one foot on the ladder and slid the rest of the way down.

"Let me show you the rest of the place. Here's my one bedroom," said Kate.

"Ugh, girlie cozy. Windows got reinforced locks and bars down the side. Good."

The living room was staged like a model home—every piece of furniture had its proper place and function. Two pictures hung over a small leather couch—one of a modern log cabin at sunrise over a sparkling lake. The other picture, from another angle, showed a rich orange-hued sunset. Denise squinted at them, checked the windows, and followed Kate into the kitchen.

"Galley kitchen, nice. Door looks good."

"Coffee, muffins, help yourself." Kate pointed to the pot and muffins.

"Nice little place. Good and solid. I hope I can have a little place like this someday."

"It's home—for me—for now. Denise, your personality is totally different when you are Dennis."

"Oh, this is me. Dennis is a character I play while in hiding. It takes a lot of work to keep this mouth of mine shut."

Denise pulled a mug off a hook and poured herself a cup of steaming black liquid. "I'll make the stairs myself. The best way to describe it would be like a library ladder on a slider. It will slide down the small wall next to your bath. I'll build shelves high-up and above your doorway. You can add your books. It will look like a little library. I'll also make a light wooden hatch for you to push up to get into your hidey hole."

"Oh, that sounds great."

"But remember, if it's shut you won't get a lot of air up there. I'll make it flush with your ceiling and swirl some paint so it will blend right in. This way I won't need help getting foldable stairs into the house. We don't want to give your stalker any clues. The light's a problem. Even with a blackout curtain, he'd be able to figure out you've made a place up here and make a plan of attack."

"Oh, I really wanted the light. I like to read in bed."

"Tough. You need to learn to go to bed and go to sleep. Read in your bedroom. It looks like you haven't been in there for a month."

"Just to get my clothes."

"Well, stop it. You need to turn lights on in your room and the living room."

"I don't understand."

"Think about it this way, Kate—you need to give him some routine. Give him a little show. In case you want to break the routine and sneak out. Think about what it would be like to watch this house, as if *you* were the creep doing it."

"I want him to leave me alone, not give him a show." Kate bit her lip and massaged her hands.

"Don't you cry, and no lip! You'll figure it out."

"Okay, but like many things that are happening in my life right now, I don't understand. I'll do what I'm told. What do I have to lose?"

Kate picked up her briefcase and opened the back door. "Please tell me one thing, Denise. Are you a battered woman in Sally's underground network?" The two women studied each other. The morning light streamed through the kitchen and danced off the cabinets. Kate persisted. "Do you know when you're leaving and where you're headed?"

"Sally said I might as well tell you—I think I'm safe for now, but I've been here longer than expected. Unless things change, I'm heading north to Nebraska, then North Dakota, then Canada. I just pray I have time to finish your job—so I best get started."

"One more thing—you believe O'Dell is coming for me?"

"Oh, girl, he's coming for you—or he'd have moved on by now. Be careful. Don't fall for any tricks. You know the famous lure is that someone will call and pretend it's the hospital calling. Someone's had an accident. The woman rushes out without thinking and gets nabbed or shot or beaten. You've got to always, always think—is this a trap?"

"Thanks, Denise, for everything. When I pick up Sic'em tonight, will you brainstorm some disguises with me?"

CHAPTER THIRTEEN

JUDGE'S CHAMBER

C lifford Baxley knew he wanted to be a judge at the age of ten, back in the days when he and another boy, Reese Matthews, had played cops and robbers—Reese assuming the part of the local sheriff and Clifford proclaiming himself the judge. The two boys, one muscled and athletic, the other tall and skinny, had realized they needed a full-time prisoner and held several auditions before finding a boy a few years older to play the part. Now, twenty-three years later, Baxley was the youngest judge in the state, and their prisoner, Dan Hand, was the Governor of the great state of Missouri.

The historic courthouse in Kingseat had undergone several changes since Clifford's appointment a year ago. A scandal had brought down Baxley's predecessor, and he was forced to resign. A phone call to the Governor had landed Baxley an emergency appointment to the bench for the 29th Circuit Court.

His first day on the job, Baxley toured the courthouse and confiscated the assessor's office. Much like the child's game, *King of the Mountain*, he simply pushed the occupants out of the office. He loved the prime location on the first floor with a beautiful view of the flowers, trees, and cars on the street, and made this office his part-time home. The assessor attempted to out-rank the tax collector and take over his office, leading the County Commissioners to hold several behind closed-door meetings in an attempt to solve the problem. The upheaval and gossip kept Baxley entertained. The judge, who reigned over three counties in rural Missouri and held court in Chariton County only part-time, kept his prime office space.

Baxley's assistant interrupted his thoughts about his boyhood exploits by intercom. "Judge, your ten o'clock is here, Reese Matthews."

"Good. Dip into petty cash, run over to the Mug Shot Café, and fetch me a cup of coffee and one of those chocolate chip muffins. Get whatever you'd like too, Marge."

"Certainly."

Marge, a slim sixty-year-old woman, owned three practical business suits: one in black, one brown, and one navy blue. Her hair was always in place and she was always at her desk. She'd kept her position after Baxley took over as judge, and after he'd taken one look at her and asked two questions: "Do you know how to run this office? Will you keep my business within these walls?" After Marge had assured him she was a woman of the highest discretion, he'd said, "You're hired."

"I'll call for Mr. Matthews when I'm ready."

"Yes, sir."

Baxley waited until he heard the friendly verbal exchange with his assistant and Reese. When he heard the front door close, he swung his door open and gestured for Matthews to come in. "Get in here, Dawg."

The two men shook hands. "Good mornin', Hard-ass. Wow, you've got everything you ever wanted, the entire town's scared of you," said Reese.

"Three counties are afraid of me. It's exhilarating."

"Thanks for helping me get my new job, Cliff."

"No problem. You know I'll owe you for the rest of my life." Tears welled in the judge's eyes as he glanced at the framed newspaper article on the wall. "It's not that you saved my life, but you saved that poor girl who was kissing me."

Reese patted his chest over his heart. "Delphina Hunt, what a heart throb. I hear she made a great teacher." He nodded at the article. "I'm surprised you admit to this mistake." The article showed a front-page picture of a Ford Mustang smashed by a train. The headline read: *Car Hit by Train—Two Teenagers Survive.*

"It hangs in all three of my offices. Few people have the chance to see the article or read the fine print where you pulled Delphina out of the car. It's on the second page. Reese, I know we've talked about this a hundred times, but you just came out of nowhere."

"I was headin' to the same smooching spot as you, dumb luck. Just like the luck that stalled your car and let your hormones get in the way of your common sense."

"Let's change the subject. Have a seat. How's your new job? You've only got one employee worth her salt, Miss Anderson."

"She's smart. Somehow, she found out I got this job shortly after I did. She was conducting a training seminar and ambushed me in front of the class."

The judge laughed. "Kate's got her ear to the ground, and she's discrete. Nothing gets by her. Courthouse walls talk. She's figured out the courthouse hierarchy and works everyone." He paused. "Well, not me."

"How long do you think it will take before someone finds out we're grade school friends? Should we wager?"

"Naw, we'd both bet on Kate. I'm mesmerized by her, Reese, but not romantically, and don't you fall for her either. You're her boss. She's wasted here in this small town. She's not afraid of me either, not afraid of sitting in jail. Your other employees get this 'deer-in-the-headlight' look in their eyes when I yell at them."

"About that, Cliff, using her as your own private investigator has to stop."

Baxley stared at Matthews. "She told you?"

"No . . . but she documented everything, and I researched her files."

Baxley laughed. "The absolute best investigation was . . . well, I think I'll let you find it."

"It's got to stop, Cliff."

"I think you should call me 'Your Honor.'"

Reese looked outside and saw Marge carrying her tray of coffee and a sack of muffins across the street.

"Anything else I need to know, Your Honor, about my new employees or my job before Marge gets here? I don't want to blow my cover with her."

Baxley peered over his glasses at Matthews. "You'll knock heads with the sheriff; police chief's an idiot. It's what the city council wants. I hate Methamphetamine. I want you to do everything you can to fight it. Whatever resources you need, let me know."

"What else do you hate, Judge?"

"City lawyers, criminals, drunk drivers, lawyers, thieves, kiss-ups, circuit clerks . . ."

"You're like the anti-Mary Poppins. She listed a few of her favorite things, you're listing a few of your most hated things."

"I also hate it when people tell me I can't do something. Miss Anderson has been invaluable to this office and my personal goals. Where do you get off telling me I can't use her as my personal P.I.?"

"Cliff, we go back a long way. We work well together. If there's any behind-the-scenes investigations, assign them to me."

"Oh, hell, I can't stay mad at you, Reese, it'll be fun having you around. Let's get a drink soon. I want to hear the story of Kate ambushing you."

"When, where?"

"I'll get a table in the back room at Dirty Sally's."

"Dirty Sally's has a back room?"

"I'll call you with details. Oh, and I hate Robert O'Dell."

Matthews stood up. "Somebody should put him in the ground."

The judge stood up, leaned on his cane, reached over the large desk, and shook Matthews' hand.

"If there's ever a problem, Your Honor, please call me. I'll be in the back of the courtroom observing my officers for the next few weeks. I hope that's all right with you?"

"As long as you leave Miss Anderson alone."

CHAPTER FOURTEEN

TWO LIVES, TWO PATHS

S usie Jones sat in the Kansas City office she shared with three other bond investigators, drumming her pink manicured nails on the steel desk, while waiting for a co-worker to hang up the phone. She needed to call Kate. Susie's life was sparkling and bright. She'd been offered a full-time job with a private security company and was dating the man of her dreams. Soon she would have her own office overlooking the famous Plaza area and would no longer have to endure the primitive, crowded conditions in the jail. No more shared phones, limited supplies, slow internet or the stench in lockup.

"Dick, my turn to use the phone—I'm tired of hearing about every bowel movement one of your children has."

Dick said a hasty goodbye to his wife, who had recently given birth to their third child. "Here ya go, Princess."

Susie pouted her pink lips, then smiled and twirled her long blonde hair. "It's the only break I have today. I'm getting all my investigations done, because I'm outta here in ten days." She threw her hands in the air,

"Whoop, whoop! Plaza lights, here I come! It will be like my own private stage."

"It's the only break I have today too, Princess."

Susie blew a kiss at Dick. She grabbed the phone and pressed speed dial to Kingseat.

"Probation and Parole, this is Kate."

"And, this is your long-lost friend, from K.C.—remember me? Come down and see me this weekend. The girls are going to see a play. It takes place in a baseball locker room and all the actors are naked! It'll be so much fun. I've bought tickets—and . . . " Susie lowered her voice, "some binoculars."

"Susie, you know I can't. Denise is bringing Sic'em Friday night. It'll be his first day home."

"But I've already bought the tickets. Oh, what did I tell you about that dog ruining all our plans?"

"I know, Susie, but it's more complicated than just the puppy. I think I'll be saying goodbye to Denise that night."

"I thought a guy named Dennis was training him."

"He was . . . well, *she* was in disguise. We've got lots to catch up on. I can't wait to see you and tell you the real story. Geez, I wish I could come down, but I can't. I promise, I'll be down soon."

"You're coming the following weekend because it's my going-away party. Mark has promised to bring a friend to meet you."

"We'll see." Kate picked up a file, her next investigation.

"You promised. This guy is flying in from New Hampshire to meet you. I've promised Mark you're a lot of fun."

"I am fun, but no one is as fun as you are, Susie. I hope they're not expecting too much. I could bring Sic'em." Kate moved her ear away from the phone.

"No, Kate. No dogs, especially a shedding, drooling, barking puppy. Board him."

Kate laughed. "Okay, okay. Listen, I need to go. I've got two interviews in the jail yet this afternoon. Call me after the play, okay? Tell me all about it."

"After the play, I'll be dancing with an actor, but I'll call you on Saturday. You better be home."

"An actor, what about your beau, Mark Larsen?"

"Mark understands me like no man ever has."

"Oh, that's an accident waiting to happen. Please tell Mark I'm looking forward to meeting his friend. I'll talk to you soon and see you next weekend."

৶   ৶   ৶

Kate climbed the stairs to her attic room and settled into her comfortable new bed. She memorized poetry lines by flashlight and liked to study Native American history and herbal remedies. She pretended she could shape-shift and talk to her spirit animals. The bedroom was a cozy haven like a climate-controlled tree house, and she was content with her thermos of herbal tea. She dreamed about what her life would be like if she had not met Robert. Even though she longed for her old life in Kansas City, she could feel herself growing away from that young college student.

The familiar lights of O'Dell's pickup cast eerie shadows across her window. Kate turned on her stomach and peered out the window through binoculars. She grabbed her calendar. A schedule emerged as she marked the days when he had shown up in his parking space. She was carefully tracking him, even as he stalked her.

≈ ≈ ≈

Kate rolled over and wiped a drool from her mouth. She'd been dreaming about having breakfast at The Corner Café and was just about ready to sink her teeth into a plate of steak and eggs when she realized her cell phone was ringing.

"Time to wake up and come get your pup."

"Who's this?" Kate rubbed her eyes and looked at the clock.

"It's Rosie, sleepyhead, come get your dog. Why don't you know who this is? Oh, I know, you haven't programmed my name into your contact list? Do it right now!"

"Okay, okay, what about my Sic'em?"

"If you still have a visitor sitting outside your house, you can stay at Sally's the rest of the night. Puppies have to be let out, you know."

Kate looked out the window. O'Dell's truck was not in the parking space.

"I'm supposed to meet Denise tomorrow night."

"Things change, Buttercup. Grab your go-bag, use this as a trial run, and get your ass over here if you want to tell Denise goodbye."

"Okay, okay. I got it. I'm coming." Kate scribbled a note in her calendar: *Two a.m. — truck gone.*

CHAPTER FIFTEEN

A WOMAN'S STORY

The white semi idled outside Dirty Sally's. Two men dressed in black hoodies and dark pants pushed dollies of stacked cartons of beer from the end of the trailer into the tavern. Almost shadows darting in the night, the men glided to and from the truck. Kate watched them for a few moments, not believing what she was seeing. She got out of her car and ran to the back of the truck, her backpack slung over her shoulder. Dennis grabbed her mid-stride and put a hand over her mouth before she screamed. "Sic'em's in the house, he's asleep. Take good care of him, he's one sweet pup."

Kate blocked his path. "You gotta leave? Will I ever see you again?"

"Nope."

"Why, why do you have to go? I don't understand." Kate stared at Dennis's face. She had not seen Denise dressed as a man since the first time they'd met. Her makeup was perfect—bushy eyebrows and a five o'clock shadow.

"Too many nosy people in this town. Your new boss, he's sharp. He got too close the other night. Sally will fill you in. We didn't wake her up—she'll find out soon enough. Stay close to her, she'll miss me and the pup."

Sally, dressed in a leopard print robe, appeared around the side of the building. "I'm up, you think I can sleep with that semi running and men unloading bootleg beer into my bar?"

Dennis hugged Sally and in his Denise voice and style said, "Thank you for everything! I owe you my life."

"It's been my pleasure, dear one. You've breathed new life into this old place."

Rosie limped up behind Sally. "We've got to go, Sal. I won't call unless I need something. Plan to be back end of next week."

"Okay, dear, drive safely." Sally hugged Dennis one last goodbye and kissed him on the cheek.

Dennis walked on as Kate stood next to Sally. He turned. "Bye, Kate! Stay safe," he said, then put up two fingers and gave Kate the peace sign.

"Peace, Denise. Send me a post card—have Rosie mail it for you."

Kate and Sally stood in the parking lot until the big truck was out of sight.

"You got any pie?" Kate asked.

"No, but I got whiskey and it looks like a fresh load of beer."

❧   ❧   ❧

Sally set up two bar glasses and poured herself a two-fingered whiskey. She nodded the bottle at Kate.

"Just a shot for me, Sally. I've got to work tomorrow and it's Criminal Law Day, my biggest day."

"You work in law enforcement, Kate, but sometimes you'll have to put on professional blinders. Since you witnessed a shipment of stolen beer and a fugitive drive off, I guess you're one of us. You can't say a word, especially to your new boss."

"A fugitive? It's time for you to loop me in, Sally. It's none of my business where you get your alcohol. But Dennis—Denise—is my friend. I need to hear her story."

"I'll tell you some of it. I can't tell you where she came from or where she's going."

"Okay, you've got a deal." Kate turned to Sally and watched her face as she spoke.

"Denise and her husband married young. The first six months were magic. They wanted to have kids right off. When she didn't get pregnant, he started to hit her. A slap now and again at first, then more full-blown beatings. About three years into the marriage, he bought a motorcycle and started running around with bikers. He had a pretty good job with a bank, but his night life crept into his day job. The bank got robbed. The feds dug up his biker life. Even though he was never charged with being an accessory to the robbery, he lost his job."

"Robert's in a biker gang."

99

Sally nodded her head. "It's one of the reasons we've been so alarmed. Most biker groups are a great asset to a community, but not all. We've suspected some women associated with that biker gang wind up being sold."

"Sold? In America? Really, Sally, it's hard to believe. How did you find out?"

"Believe it. Polite people don't talk about it, but it happens in America today. Do you want to hear the rest?"

"Of course. Please, go on."

"Denise had a rich housewife's life. She went to lunch with friends, had her hair and nails done. It's a life hard to give up, especially when you don't have any job skills. When her husband still had his job, he would win her back with promises and presents. After he lost his job, he would find her and drag her back. He started handcuffing her to the bed—then beat her because supper wasn't on the table."

Sally paused and took a drink of the warm liquid. "One night, he came home, drunk and mean. He handed her a gun, 'Shoot me, if you don't love me,' he said.

"She shot him—twice. Chained to the bed, needing medical attention, she somehow got out of her restraints."

Kate shook her head, "Damn, I wish I'd known."

"Why? She didn't want your pity."

Kate's face turned red as if she'd been slapped. "I can't pretend to know what it's like to take a beating. Robert only hit me once, but I'll never forget that feeling—even though it was only for a few seconds—that feeling when I realized I was at his mercy. I just wish I hadn't acted so juvenile with Denise, as if she were playing a game like Susie does."

"Unfortunately, her husband survived. Denise was convicted of armed criminal action. She spent three years behind bars. Now she has her ex-husband and the motorcycle gang after her. She's been on the run two years."

Sally paused and Kate spoke. "Are you going to tell me about Sister Anne and the convent?"

"Sister Anne is still at the convent in Leavenworth. There's another group of women who live very close to her. We call them 'sisters'— it's their own disguise. They aren't nuns—Christians, pagans, witches—maybe." Sally laughed. "It's the closest safe house we have. Denise won't be going there tonight—she's on a cross country trucker haul."

"Did she have to leave because of Reese?"

"No, she had to leave; she'd overstayed. He was here the other night in the back room with the judge. He was very curious about the premises and the back yard. She'd been here long enough. We get a sense about this."

"The judge? Reese was in the back room with the judge?"

"Yes, Kate. They are grade school pals who grew up in Jeff City. The governor grew up with them."

"What? Wow, I'm getting lessons tonight. I guess that explains how Reese got his job, and why he's so nosey about O'Dell and O'Dell's job with the governor."

"Thick as thieves, they are. Let's try to get some sleep, dear."

"Can I get Sic'em and bring him in?"

"No, but I'll walk with you over to Denise's house to see him. I guess I'm going to have to start calling the place the 'B&B.' I'll show you the alarm system and the security we have in place." Sally reached under the bar and pulled out a present wrapped in gold paper. The package looked like a jewelry box, long and thin. "Denise left this for you."

"She left me a present?"

"Yeah, open it."

Kate tore the wrapping paper off the box. Inside was a small stiletto in a sheath. The initial "S" was burned into the leather.

"It wraps around your thigh. It's a present from 'The Sisterhood.' One day, you'll be giving one of these to another woman."

"Does that mean I'll be entering the sisterhood and on the run? I hope not, Sally."

"Like I said, Kate, we have a sense about these things. It literally means, you've been tapped or you're next. You've been handed the baton, so to speak. This is my twenty-fifth dagger—I haven't been wrong yet."

CHAPTER SIXTEEN

COUNTY JAIL

Matthews rounded the corner of the hallway in the Chariton County Jail and stopped in front of Kate's cell. She wore a red designer suit— her black silk blouse matched her heels. Legs crossed, her hands locked around her knees, she stared at the wall. When she saw him, she stood up, like a little Christmas soldier. "Did you bring me a good book?"

"A fine mess you've got us into, Ollie." Reese grinned at her.

"You should see it from my side of the bars. Not exactly what I had planned for this evening."

"What were you thinking?"

"I was thinking that kid shouldn't be sent to prison."

"What happened to your three thousand dollars for bail money? I thought that was your plan."

"I found out I'll lose three hundred dollars, and that they can keep my money until the judge releases it. I can't really afford to do that right now. My old boss would've let me sit in jail—I decided to see what my new boss will do. Will I get paid?"

"You're gonna have to apologize."

"Do you think it will build character and add to my street cred?" Kate sat back down. "You're gonna have to find a way to save that kid."

"You're not being realistic. He's the judge and you can't save them all."

"Maybe I can save this one."

"First of all, was there a reason you were late to court? Some night life going on to make you too busy to show up on time?"

Kate stood up and put her hands on her hips. "I was *not* late for court. Who told you I was late?"

"Calm down, Kate. I'm trying to understand why the judge would throw you in jail."

"Why, because you know him so well, did your grade school buddy surprise you?" Kate's face turned red as she fumed at her boss.

"No, because I thought you two got along splendidly. Speaking of trivia, didn't he represent you when you were just a teen?"

"Oh. He seems to have forgotten he liked me."

"Tell me what happened."

"We had a sixteen-year-old boy in court this morning. We did a pre-sentence investigation on him. He was adjudicated as an adult. Why did the judge do that?"

"I can't speak for the judge. He must've had his reasons. I remember the investigation—the kid broke into a gas station and a clothing store."

"Yes, that's the one. His folks threw him out of the house. He didn't have a coat and he didn't have any money. Judge Baxley released him on his own recognizance— but warned the boy that 'he better not see him again until court day.'"

"Go on." Reese stepped closer to the bars.

"Well, the kid was not too bright, and he was hungry. He broke into a house and stole some cookies. The police followed his tracks that led to a cardboard box where he was living under the bridge on Third Street. I got called in to do the investigation. The judge didn't like my—our—recommendation, because the kid had gotten himself re-arrested. He sent him to prison for seven years. Seven years! He's sixteen years old."

"Did you really say, 'he stole *cookies* for God's sake'?"

"Yes. I know it was disrespectful. I suppose I deserve being held in contempt."

"You're gonna have to apologize to the judge."

"I think you should call the attorney general's office and tell them you have a bond investigator sitting in jail. Call your friend the governor."

"Kate, this isn't the time for you to make a stand. Use the three thousand dollars you have stuffed in your bra, or apologize—it's getting late, the judge may already be gone. Yes, I've known Baxley since we were kids. He's not going to give in. In fact, he's so mad, you may have to be reassigned."

"Well, I think I'll survive a night in jail."

"You can't do that boy any good by sitting in jail."

"Maybe not, but you can't let this sentence stand, you have to do something. Please, Reese. He's only sixteen." Kate knew she was pleading, but her poker face had taken a hike.

"It's done. Can't you see that? Baxley isn't going to reverse his order. The best thing we can do is to work within our own system. You know it better than I do. Maybe we can get the kid into a treatment program on our end. Maybe after treatment, Baxley will release him—*if* you apologize."

"It's my fault then?"

"Yes, it's your fault. You get too personally involved with every case. Your snide mouth got you thrown in jail."

"The judge is a bully. I've been sent to my room without any supper plenty of times. Who knows, I might sleep better in solitary."

"And, you're okay using that toilet?"

Kate turned around and saw the filthy toilet, the stains and mold crawling out of the hole, and the small dirty seat. She wrinkled her nose and looked down at her tight red skirt.

"Yeah, that skirt's gonna be a problem. See that camera? While you're doing a shimmy with your skirt, it will be captured on film and sent to other sheriff's offices. And—what about Sic'em? Who's gonna feed your dog?"

"I'll admit, my skirt might be a problem. I'll apologize for my rude behavior."

"Deputy!" Matthews yelled.

A portly deputy dressed in brown brought keys to the cell.

"Let's get her across the street, before the judge leaves for the day."

CHAPTER SEVENTEEN

PRISONER

K ate unlocked the back door, Sic'em by her side. "Everything okay boy? Let's check it out." The growing dog sniffed his way through the house. He barked in each room, letting her know it was safe. She patted him on the head and gave him his treat.

Kate's house, once a cozy cottage with quality furniture placed exactly in the right place, now looked more like a gym—a red punching bag hung from the ceiling and a black kick bag swung on a large spring. The kickbag was in a perpetual state of motion. Every time Kate walked by it, she punched or kicked it. Sic'em thought it was his new toy and swung it and barked at it.

Kate began her routine, first stretches, then kicks to the bag, then punches, followed by sit-ups and push-ups. After forty-five minutes, she paused and drank some water.

I'm like an inmate—a prisoner in my own home. All I do is work and work-out. I might as well be in jail—except I have a better toilet.

107

"You're a good boy." The dog perked up, came over, and sat next to Kate. "You're *such* a good boy. What would I do without you?"

"Okay, Sic'em, here I go." Kate sprang to standing position and kicked the bag in the circle that represented O'Dell's head. "No!" she screamed. "No." Kate kicked the groin circle. "No!" She punched the face.

Her furious workout lasted another forty-five minutes and then she folded like a kerchief falling to the floor.

"Okay, Sic'em. It's time to call Pops."

Kate pulled the phone off the small table by the sofa and called her grandfather.

"There you are," Pops said.

"And there *you* are. How are you? How'd you know it was me?"

"We got caller ID. I decided it would be handy to know who was calling us. Sometimes we ignore the people from the country club. Do you have it?"

"Yes, Pops, I like it too. How's Grandma?"

"She's mean as ever."

Kate laughed. "I hope she can hear you." She petted Sic'em's head and tugged on his ears.

"What's new with you, Katrina?"

"Sic'em and I were just training and I'm planning to grab a bite to eat. What did you have for supper?"

"I grilled a couple of fillets. Are you applying for law schools?"

"It's not the time to apply, Pops." She shifted on the floor.

The old man cleared his throat. She could hear a Frank Sinatra song playing in the background. "Katrina, just go. You know we have a college fund for you."

"Yes, thank you. I wanted a little more court experience." *If he knew I had spent a couple of hours in jail this afternoon, he'd probably have a stroke.*

"Well, now you have it—you need to get away."

"It's hard to explain, but I don't think running will help me. He'll just follow me. I've got support here. I'm licensed to carry a gun. I'd be all alone on a college campus, a perfect target. He followed me here."

"Pops, let's not quarrel. Okay? You two have a lovely evening, I bet there's a great Hallmark movie on tonight—early Christmas specials this week, you know."

"Yes, we have it all set to watch. Thanks for calling."

Pops hung up the phone and Kate felt the familiar grind in the pit of her stomach. *Pops, if it only were that easy. Go to law school. He doesn't understand I may have to disappear like Denise.*

"Sic'em—my world keeps getting smaller and smaller as he isolates me from everyone." *Trapped like a butterfly in a jar, beating her wings. How many other women feel like this? I can't wait to see Susie this weekend.*

Kate peered through the telescoping porthole and saw O'Dell sitting in his car, drinking his beer. He picked up his binoculars and looked straight at the house. Kate jumped as if he could see her. Her heart raced as she turned, leaned against the door, and then slid to the floor. The dog pounced on her. "It'll be okay, won't it, Sic'em?"

Her phone rang and she jumped. She picked it up and said, "What do you want?" The caller hung up.

How can I make him go away? I'm like a caged bird with the door open, too afraid to go out and explore the world.

Kate crawled into her little attic space. Sic'em whined in his crate. "Go to sleep, Sic'em." Hearing Kate's voice, the puppy crawled out of his open crate and circled the stairs. "Lay down, Sic'em." He obeyed. She dozed off to sleep.

◈   ◈   ◈

Kate's cell phone rang, and O'Dell's familiar voice came over the line. "You're going to do exactly what I say. Meet me at Dirty Sally's bar on October sixteenth. I'm having a birthday party. Wear that red suit. Cut a few slits up the side—or *I will*." He laughed into the phone. "You love that old man, don't you? You want him safe, right? Think of the ways I could kill him."

She hung up the phone, slid down the ladder, and headed straight toward the punching bag. Punch, kick, punch. *You're a dead man, Robert O'Dell*, Kate screamed at the black bag. "Don't you dare threaten my family!"

CHAPTER EIGHTEEN

WITCHES

Denise's story had ignited a primal chord within Kate—a spiritual call to the sisterhood of battered women.

The contraband beer, unloaded the night Denise left, was from the local brewery. Any out-of-date cans of beer were stacked and then crushed in the warehouse loading dock. Years ago, Sally made a deal with the distributor. She cooked for the Missouri University homecoming tailgate party. In turn, he would deliver pallets of beer. She couldn't *sell* it, but she could make beer bread with it. Bratz and beer bread made for a great tailgate party. Sally and her waitresses received large tips from the elite clients of the brewery. Everyone won.

Sally ferried most of the cases over to the Sisterhood in Leavenworth and they made beer bread for farmer's markets and private parties, mostly sporting events. Kate became involved in the bread-making process. A large steel bowl, self-rising flour, a little sugar, and a can of beer. She stirred the mixture until it formed a ball and then placed it into a loaf pan. Forty-five minutes later, she brushed the loaf with butter and re-inserted it into the oven.

111

The aroma of the bread sifted through the bar, and Sally sauntered up behind Kate.

"You're spending a lot of time here—not that I mind, but I'm worried about you. You're thin as a rail."

"It's all muscle." Kate raised her fist to her face in a body builder pose.

Sally laughed as Kate struck another pose and made a grimace.

Kate eyed the oven. "I can get five loaves into the oven, but I can't get a six pack. I've tried and tried, it just won't hold six loaves."

"Talk to me, Kate. What's on your mind? You've got the world's problems on your shoulders."

"O'Dell threatened to kill Pops. He's demanded I come here on October sixteenth for his birthday party. He wants me to wear my red suit."

"Oh, that bastard. He's so brazen and out of control." Sally faced Kate and grabbed her by the shoulders. "Listen to me. We would never stop looking for you, do you hear me?"

"I'm not going to let it come to that. It sounds like I have a little time."

"It could be a trap. He might be lulling you into a sense of safety. That's a long time for a cat to play with a mouse."

"What does that mean?"

"Like a cat will play with a mouse before he finally kills it.

"The point is, just because he's leading you to believe he's waiting until October sixteenth doesn't mean he won't grab you before then. You have to tell Theodore," warned Sally.

"I know, I know, but he'll be so disappointed in me. How do I tell him?"

"Your grandfather wasn't always an old man. He knows how to take precautions. Nobody dared rob your grandfather's store."

"I never really thought about it. Are you saying Pops has like—mob connections?"

"Connections—yes, he has connections. Sometimes I forget how young you are. When do you think O'Dell will park his truck outside your house again?"

"I think tomorrow night. You're not going to let me know anything more about Pops, are you?"

"Go home, get some sleep. I have some calls to make and a party to plan."

≈ ≈ ≈

Kate watched out the front window of her house. A blue Mazda parked outside the front of her house. Four women sat inside. Kate opened the front door, and the women, dressed in black, shooed her back inside. A red Ford F-150 drove into her yard and parked in the side yard to the east. A small Honda with four more women parked out back. In a few minutes, Sally's pink Cadillac, a remnant of her career as a Mary Kaye saleswoman, flew around to the south side of the house.

Sic'em barked at each vehicle and ran back and forth from window to window. "It's okay, boy. I think they're friends. It looks like they parked in the four directions:

north, south, east, and west." Kate looked at the dog as if he were a small person. "It's a witch's ritual. I'm not sure I like this."

With his face just inches away from hers, the dog gave Kate a slobbery lick. He turned in circles and barked again.

"Sit, Sic'em. No. They're friends. Friends, Sic'em. Aren't you glad we're on this dead-end street with only one close neighbor?"

A shadow passed the window and rapped on the front door. Kate opened it to Sally who was dressed in a black filmy gown with a black hat. "Say goodbye to that red suit."

"It cost me two hundred dollars!"

Sic'em recognized Sally and stood up, wagging his tail. She walked into Kate's bedroom and opened the closet. "Make some iced tea, do you have any food?"

"Not a lot. I've got beer bread, chocolate, veggies, and some fruit. Tea? Is this a tea party? What about booze?"

"Oh, that's perfect, almost like you knew we were coming. Make some tea, not everyone drinks alcohol, Kate." Sally threw her head back and laughed. "Don't you like a good witch's party?"

"Umm, no . . . not really . . . uh, I don't know, never had one. What are they doing out there, are they building a fire? There's city ordinances against fires after dark."

"I've taken care of it." Sally flipped through Kate's closet and found the red designer suit with the short tight skirt. The plastic bag clung to the jacket in a futile effort to save it from destruction. "Oh, Kate, this is beautiful, such a shame."

"Hey, wait! Let me save the blouse—I can wear it with other things." Kate peeled the plastic off the suit and slid the blouse out from underneath the jacket.

Sally hurried into the living room and handed the suit out the front door. Four women stood under the streetlight, dressed in black. Some of them wore decorated hats. They chanted something Kate strained to hear.

"Darkest night, silver moon. Witches, witches, return to the rune."

They cut the jacket with pinking shears into a long rope, much like peeling an apple. They held the rope high above their heads. The women cut the skirt and held it, too, above their heads. Soon the other eight women joined the first four, and they formed a long line, strung together with the red-suit rope. Sally was the end of the train as they circled the house.

Kate sank onto the yoga mat, and the puppy pounced into her lap. "Well, there goes two hundred bucks. What do you think, boy?" *Oh, well, I'm not going to need it where I'm going.*

The chanting stopped and Kate jumped up and ran to the window. "Oh, this oughta be good. Sic'em, they're marching up the road."

Twelve women with big sticks, chanting and banging the ground, marched up the road. Kate grabbed Sic'em's leash and followed them up the street toward O'Dell's truck.

When the women were a half block from the truck, O'Dell backed out of the parking place and drove straight at the females in his path. As he got near them, they were forced closer to the side of the road. A few jumped the ditch. Only Sally stood her ground. Sic'em yanked the leash out of Kate's hand and charged the car, biting and chewing at the tires.

Kate chased after the dog.

O'Dell yelled out the window at Kate, "I'll see you soon, sweetheart."

❧   ❧   ❧

Kate and the "witches" returned to her house, laughing at their antics. The women pulled more food out of their cars, and they sat around the fire and told little stories. Sally brought out marshmallows, chocolate and graham crackers and they made s'mores. One woman stood out from the rest—she seemed to be two sizes larger than Kate and her hair was flaming red. A natural storyteller, she kept them laughing with stories of her travels.

With these strong women, Kate felt safe and like she belonged in something she didn't quite understand, but found connecting and supportive. The party broke up at the stroke of midnight. A woman threw water on the fire, the smoke turned grey, and sparks flew toward the heavens to join the stars. The women stopped what they were doing to watch.

Dishes were whisked into the house and trash thrown away.

Rosie came out of the darkness and took Kate by the shoulder. "Denise is in Calgary, Canada. She should be safe there, Kate."

"Thanks for telling me. I know you weren't supposed to do that."

"No problem. Good party, Kate."

A sleepy Sic'em circled a couple times and returned to his bed on the ground.

"C'mon, Sally, we're escorting you home." The group surrounded the older woman and walked her to her pink Cadillac.

The storyteller hung back from the group. "My name is Maureen Thompson and if that crazy judge throws you in jail again, here's my card, give me a call." She handed Kate a card. Kate looked at it and saw that the woman was an attorney. When she looked up, the woman was sweeping to her black Volvo.

Once they were gone, Kate felt all alone.

CHAPTER NINETEEN

SIC'EM

Kate pulled into her driveway shortly after five o'clock. She couldn't wait to see Sic'em. The puppy was the one spot of light in her dreary life. He now weighed fifty pounds, and he barked like a big dog—because he was one. She loved to run with him. Denise had warned her about making Sic'em a pet, but in a very short time, Kate's entire world had come to revolve around the puppy.

She bounded up the steps like a little girl with a new cherry lollipop, stretched up on her tiptoes, and peered through the small window in the back door of her yellow cottage. She expected to see the dog staring up at her, with his brown eyes that matched hers in color, and his paws raised against the door.

He wasn't there.

Kate banged the door with the palm of her hand. "Sic'em! Come here, boy." Kate peered around the kitchen and saw him lying on the floor next to his doggie door. "No, no, Sic'em! Sic'em! Bark! Oh, please bark."

She tried to unlock the door. Her hands shook, and she couldn't work the lock. *Kick the door in, just kick the damn door in. Oh, my God—it's too late.* She stood on her tippy toes and again peered in the window. This time she could see white foam running out of the dog's mouth. She could see he wasn't breathing.

She sat down on the porch step. *Not Sic'em. What have I done, what have I done to you? My poor puppy.*

She heard the familiar sound of O'Dell's pickup as he pulled around the corner. Rousing from her grief, she jumped up, grabbed her pistol, and pointed it low. She side-stepped to the side of the house, ready for O'Dell to come around the corner. She breathed in and out slowly, and listened, trying to locate where the truck had gone. *It's stopped in the middle of the street out front. Wait...*

It seemed like an eternity, but she heard the truck back up the street. She sat down on the steps and laid the weapon next to her leg. *What am I going to do now? What will I do without Sic'em?*

Kate dug in her purse and retrieved her phone. She called Ron Davis.

"Hi Kate, you going on a ride-along with me tonight? It's my first night back."

"No, Ron, I need your help. Can you come by?"

"Sure. What is it, Kate?"

"He's killed my puppy. He's killed my beautiful dog. I'm too upset to even get into the house."

"Kate—surely not—how did he get in? Never mind, I'll be right there. Don't touch anything. We'll need to take prints."

"I know, Ron, but we won't find anything." Kate put her head in her arms and cried, big hiccupping sobs.

"Kate, Kate, are you still there? I'm calling Matthews."

She pressed the phone back to her ear. "All right. I think that's all right."

❧ ❧ ❧

Ron pulled up at the back of the house in his patrol car. He was still sore from his prostate surgery and his duty belt hung heavy. He saw Kate sitting against the house, and he shook his head. He got out of the car and tried to sit on the step with her, but pain got in his way. "Kate, give me your keys." She looked up at him; tears and mascara stained her face. She wiped her eyes and dug in her pants pocket for her keys.

"Thanks for coming."

"No problem, sweetheart. Listen, I've got a couple officers coming. They won't be here long. They'll take prints, but probably nothing else—it should be a felony, but it's not. There won't be much of an investigation. Do you have something, a sheet, maybe a blanket I can cover him with, so you won't have to see him this way?"

"No—it's mine to do. I think I'll go and get a shovel out of the garage and take him to the cabin."

"Kate, that's a long drive from here. And O'Dell might follow you—it's too predictable. It's an obvious trap."

"I don't care—I really don't care anymore."

Ron let himself in the kitchen and saw the poor pup laying on the floor. There was foam coming from his mouth flecked with pieces of meat. *I've seen enough—*

Kate heard the sound of a familiar truck come around the house again, this time almost colliding with the Jeep Wrangler driven by Matthews. The truck drove over into the shoulder, avoiding a collision.

Matthews got out of his truck, walked up to Kate, and hugged her.

"Get off me, you big lug."

"Okay, no problem. I'm going in the house." He shook hands with Ron. "Thanks for calling me, Ron. Damn shame, beautiful dog. Somebody oughta kill that bastard."

"Well, didn't have much choice on who to call. She can't bury him by herself, and I'm on duty. She says she wants to bury him out on the family farm. She shouldn't do it alone. She might need company."

"I'll take care of it. What do you think happened here?"

The cop pointed toward the doggie door. "It looks like someone pushed open the door just enough to insert a hotdog through the slot. Rat poison would be my guess. Hard way to die."

⋞ ⋞ ⋞

O'Dell sat in his pickup and took a swig of Budweiser. He picked up the binoculars. *I hope the local cops come and ask questions about the dead dog. She's home, why don't I hear anything? I want her in the house. Damn it! I want to hear her scream and cry.* His cell phone rang.

"What in the hell's wrong with you?" He recognized the sheriff's voice.

"Cousin, what do you mean?" He crushed the empty beer can.

"Get the hell out of there if you don't want to spend some nights in jail."

"I'd be out before my birthday. That's all that matters."

"Listen Robert, I can't help you anymore, you understand? I've got her crazy boss breathing down my neck and they're pushing for a task force to investigate you and your biker gang. Just leave the girl alone. She's not worth it."

"Oh, she's worth it. Trust me she's worth it. I'll do what you say tonight. Soon you won't have to worry about it anymore."

"What in the hell does that mean?"

O'Dell turned the key in the ignition. "I'm leaving, Sheriff. Don't worry about me."

He drove around Kate's house one more time. The police car was parked in her driveway. He caught a glimpse of her in her black suit. *I love that suit. I want to hear her scream—with pleasure—with pain. She'll learn to love it.* He looked up and saw a Jeep Wrangler headed straight for him. He swerved in a near-miss collision, swerved again, missed the ditch, and sped away.

∽ ∽ ∽

It was dark when Matthews pulled up in front of the gate to Theodore Anderson's property. Kate got out of the vehicle, unlocked the gate, and opened it for the Jeep. The headlights swung around, caught the young woman, and paused as if they could not look away. She wore a state-issued ball cap with "Trainer" stamped on the bill. Her hair was pulled through the back and her ponytail curled down the front of her sweatshirt. Her eyes were puffy and swollen. The Jeep moved through the gate, and Kate pushed it the rest of the way open, hooking it on a post. She opened the car door and jumped into the passenger seat.

The moon shown bright, and stars poked through the sky like nosy neighbors in a big city. Two geese honked in loud protest at the intruders. Kate pointed, "Pull around the cabin, Reese. I'll find a place to bury him in the hayfield near the lake. Sic'em loved the lake and liked to chase the geese." Her shoulders shook as she attempted not to cry.

Reese parked, got out of the vehicle, and opened the hatch. He stayed quiet and resisted all temptation to reach for her. He removed a shovel, handed it to her, and grabbed another. The two made short work of the horrendous chore. Finishing at the same time, they walked silently to the Jeep, and pulled out the blanketed dog, Kate's companion, carrying him together to his early grave. They buried him, then stood looking at the pile of dirt.

"I wish I knew how to help you . . . "

"I know. Thank you, Reese, for being here. This would have been so much worse without a friend."

He placed his hand over his heart. "I've made it to your 'friend' list? I'm teasing, I'm teasing."

Kate attempted to smile. "Would you mind sitting on the dock with me for a few minutes, or do you need to get back?"

"Sure, let me get a blanket." He retrieved a blanket from the Jeep and followed her down the walkway of the rickety dock. They spread the blanket and sat down cross-legged. He handed her a flask, and she sipped on the whiskey.

Kate was the first to speak. "Stars are full out tonight. This may be one of the last beautiful nights before it gets cold."

"I don't mind winter. I love to walk in the woods and see my breath in early morning. Why did you name him Sic'em?"

"Oh, I didn't. I mean, well—the theory was if I needed help, and I yelled 'Sic'em!' an intruder would think a dog was charging. He would take his eyes off me and look at the dog. I would have enough time to react, grab a weapon, and charge the intruder with a big dog by my side. It's brilliant really, but I can't take credit for it."

"Good strategy, I guess—a little odd, maybe."

"I've worked out most of my life's problems on this old dock, boys punching me, girls making fun of me, but this problem is too big."

"Things usually work themselves out, even when you think they won't."

"He killed my puppy."

"I know, Kate. I'm sorry." He pulled her close to him and let her cry on his shoulder. Sobs racked her body. She found herself sitting on his lap entwined in his arms. They fit together like perfect puzzle pieces. A cloud floated by, darkening the moon and dimming the stars, giving the couple complete privacy.

CHAPTER TWENTY

MURDER ON THE MIND

Premeditated murder. The words repeated and spiraled in Kate's mind as she studied the *Farmer's Almanac,* picking a night with a sliver of a moon. She circled October fourteenth on her calendar in red ink. Could she do it? The law would not be on her side. She was not in imminent danger. There was no defense. She had no proof he had been terrorizing her.

Kate prepared and planned her steps. Before breakfast and at lunch every day she snuck across the vacant lot, memorizing every rock, every step. She played it in her head—him sitting in the truck—her shooting him dead. There was no other way. The relentless calls and threats had continued until she had finally disconnected her home phone and changed her cell phone number. She needed quiet. The police and the prosecutor were unable or unwilling to arrest O'Dell for harassment.

He would kill her grandfather just like he'd killed Sic'em. Sally would do everything she could to protect her at the bar, but it wouldn't be enough.

Kate pulled into the driveway of her grandparents' house. The couple took great pride in their home. They had spent two years talking with architects and builders to get the house the way they both wanted it. The design of the front porch was the best feature. They had studied the plans spread over the kitchen table every night and talked and re-arranged furniture into the night. Kate, five years old at the time, had played with Barbie and Ken and pretended the dolls were her parents before they died in a plane crash.

Kate slid open the glass door to their dining area. "Anybody home?"

Her grandmother played solitaire on the computer at the other end of the living room, but she couldn't see her grandfather. "Pops, are you home?"

Pops's recliner clanked as he lowered his feet and she saw his white head appear as he stood slowly and turned around. "Katrina, what a surprise. What are you doing here?"

Grandma Helen turned and looked up from the computer, closed the game, and rearranged her walker. She began the slow process of standing up and trying to make her legs work.

"Pops, I'm sorry to wake you."

"It's okay, I wasn't asleep. Can you have a drink with us?"

Kate laughed. "Pops it's just a little after one o'clock. I've got to go back to work. I just had a question for you."

Grandma Helen said, "Sit down, Katrina, sit down."

127

The three positioned themselves around the oval table, which had been the framework for family dinners and many games of cards. Kate said, "I've decided to take a little trip and check out some colleges. It wouldn't be until next weekend, but I wanted to tell you I will be gone—for a while." Her voice cracked, but she continued. "I'm taking a vacation, maybe a couple of weeks. I just wanted to—well, thank you for encouraging me to go to law school and umm . . . everything you've done for me."

Pops stared at Kate. "Stop beating around the bush and acting like a little girl. Of course, we want you to go to law school. How much money do you need?"

"I don't need any money, Pops."

Grandma Helen spoke. "Theodore, get my purse, let me give her some cash."

"Grandma, really, I don't need any money. I just wanted to see you and tell you about my decision."

Pops said, "Nonsense, we got cash the other day. I'm giving you some money—you might need a down payment for an apartment or something."

"Okay, thank you, but also, Pops—uh, do you still set the security system in your house? And, you both wear the First Alert necklaces, right?"

Grandma Helen pointed at the keypad. "We've been setting it since you had the trouble with that man."

"Would you do me a favor and be extra careful? Those alarm buttons are made to be used. If you suspect an intruder, please push the alarm and tell the operator to call the police."

"Katrina, what's this about? Why are you so troubled?"

"Pops, I'm sorry. I got involved with a very dangerous man. He's made threats.

"What kind of threats?" Grandma Helen asked.

"He's made threats against you, Pops."

Pops waved a hand in dismissal. "I don't care, Katrina. Go live your life. Don't worry about us—we'll be fine."

"Theodore, go load the shotguns right now. We'll feel better if you get them loaded."

The old man rose and shuffled in his slippers across the carpet. Kate followed. He stopped at the hall closet and opened the door. A tall shotgun stood in the corner. "Get that box of shells." He pointed to the high shelf in the closet.

Kate stood on her tiptoes and grabbed the box of shells. Pops picked up the shotgun and pointed it toward the floor to load it. Studying her grandfather, she realized he could no longer reach the shells. Time had passed. Her grandfather was an old man.

"Pops, let's find a safe place to put this."

"Just lay it over the chair by the door—pointing toward the door like in the old days."

"Pops, that's not safe. Put it here in the corner." She pointed at the corner by the door. "You'll have to be fast."

She followed her grandfather into the bedroom. "Katrina, you made this mess with this man; you need to clean it up."

"I know. I'm so sorry." Tears welled in Kate's eyes.

They loaded the shotgun in the bedroom. "Do you need anything moved so Grandma can stay out of the line of fire?"

"Oh, we have our plan. We've let down our guard over the years. We don't keep a lot of cash in the house like we used to. She'll head to the bathroom with the pistol. Lord help the man that opens that door."

Pops opened the small door in the side table near the bed, revealing a safe. "Katrina, get that pistol out for me."

Kate got down on her knees and peered into the safe. "*Not much cash?* Pops, there's a *bunch* of money in here."

"Pull a couple of stacks out."

Katrina obeyed and handed the money to her grandfather. She stood up, examining the gun. "Pops, this .357 hasn't been cleaned in years."

Pops pointed at the safe, "Well, there should be a gun cleaning kit in there, get it out. I'll clean it tomorrow."

Kate retrieved the kit. "Should I lock the safe?"

"Oh, never mind that, we forgot the combination years ago. Take that money, Katrina. You might need it."

"Pops, it's all right, I'm selling my car and my house. I'll have plenty of money."

"Like that gun, we haven't seen that money in years. There should be a couple thousand dollars there. Use it to set up your college apartment."

"Pops . . ."

"You need to be fiercer and smarter, remember?"

Tears filled her eyes again. "He says he's gonna kill you."

"Stop that whining, Katrina, only babies cry. If he comes here, he'll be sorry."

"O'Dell's a trained killer."

The old man stood up a little taller, "So am I."

Maybe I am too. Kate left her grandparents' house with a new determination.

CHAPTER TWENTY-ONE

WITNESS

K ate lay in her loft bed and watched through her binoculars, waiting for O'Dell's pickup to arrive. Her go-bag, packed with t-shirts, jeans and cash, was stuffed in the trunk of her car. She liked the little blue Mazda, a "soccer mom" car, but she knew not to get attached to it. She would swap it out somewhere in Iowa. She hoped to be in Des Moines tonight. *What if he doesn't show?*

Truck lights passed her window and, as predicted, O'Dell circled the block to check out the vehicle in the driveway. Kate pressed her new phone-controlled home defense system and turned on the kitchen light. She looked through her binoculars and watched O'Dell park his truck. He popped a beer. She pushed another button, and the light went off. She clicked again—the television came on. She turned up the volume.

I've got ya now, Buddy—just like watching television, isn't it, Robert? Kate crept down the stairs and slipped into her big fluffy bathrobe. She pulled her hair up into a towel as if she had just taken a shower. She believed he could see her silhouette with the lights on. She sat on the couch and waited with the drop gun in her lap, while watching a re-run of *Ally McBeal,* her plan rolling over and over in her mind as she waited. At ten thirty, she turned off the light, slid off the couch onto the floor, and shed the robe.

Dressed in dark camo, Kate crab-walked across the floor through the living room, then the kitchen. She crawled out the doggie door and hid beside the house. Like a mere shadow, she crept sideways from tree to tree.

Kate moved—waited—listened. Moved—waited—listened. She had checked and rechecked her route and knew every step of the way. She stopped, stretched out belly flat, and peered into the darkness, then rolled over on her back and looked up at the sky. The darkness caressed her like a sleeping bag as she tried to calm her heart. It beat so fast she thought she might take flight like a helicopter. A few stars winked at her in the blackness of the night sky. She wanted to stay in this protection. She rolled back over and peered up at the truck parked about twenty yards away.

She laid her head on the ground. *I don't think I can shoot him, but what am I going to do? He will kill Pops.* "Our Father who art in heaven . . . ." Kate mumbled the rote prayer which then turned into a silent chant to her Native American ancestors. *If there is any other way, please show it to me now.* A twig snapped, and Kate's heart stopped. She raised her head in a slow-moving yoga stretch and searched the blackness.

O'Dell took another swig of beer, turned, and looked out the passenger window of his truck.

A figure, dressed in black, emerged from the cover of a nearby tree. Kate stifled a scream—hand over mouth. *What the hell is going on?*

Flash. Bang-bang.

Oh my God. Someone's shot O'Dell.

Kate's gaze followed the shooter down the street, and she stared as the figure disappeared through the alley toward the police station. *Call 911, call 911*, Kate's thoughts screamed in her head. *No, you can't call.* She lay frozen to the ground. *That was a double tap. Cops are trained to shoot twice. I wonder if he's dead.*

A siren wailed, then stalled and wailed again.

I've got to get the hell out of here.

Kate sprung up in one movement and ran straight across the field, bounded over a fence, and across her yard. She put her key in the back door, but was shaking too badly to unlock it. She raised her boot towards the doorknob and with one adrenaline-filled kick, cracked the door frame. She kicked again, stepped back, and kicked again. The door finally gave way in splintering defeat. She grabbed her keys and her new purse, and reached in the cubby for her duty weapon.

It's not here. Where is it? Where is it? Did I leave it at work? . . . She picked up a chair and threw it across the room in a fit of rage. Her cell phone followed the chair and crashed into pieces. She sprinted down the steps, jumped into her car, and slipped a cotton print dress over her head. She pulled her ponytail through the back of a pink ball cap and roared out of her driveway in reverse, pitched the car into drive, and drove with no headlights for half of a block.

Sally's words roared in her head. "If anything changes, head for the convent." Kate added a pair of black librarian-style glasses and headed straight for the convent, ninety miles west.

Change of plans, Sisters, you're getting a visitor tonight. Her new name is Jane Jones.

CHAPTER TWENTY-TWO

CRIME SCENE

Matthews pulled up the yellow, crime-scene tape and ducked under the barrier. He scanned the area and noted the sheriff barking orders at deputies about roadblocks. The chief of police was listening to Ron Davis. Matthews walked over to the pickup and stared at the body inside, then walked around the truck and glanced across the field at Kate's yellow cottage, following the direct line of sight into her living room. All the lights were on and the blinds were open.

The police chief walked over to Matthews. "I think she just snapped, walked up to the truck, smiled, and shot him. What do you think, Matthews?"

"Chief, I'm trying not to deck you, so I would watch your mouth around me. That her duty weapon in that bag?"

"Yeah, she must've really snapped to leave her weapon at the scene." The chief stepped back, realizing his mistake.

Matthews glared at him. "You're such an idiot. Where'd you find it?"

"There—in the passenger seat."

"You think Kate—the Kate we know—would plan a murder and then just drop her weapon in the passenger seat of the truck?"

The police chief answered, "That *is* what I'm saying. I think she lost it. I think she just walked up, had her weapon at the ready. Maybe he said something to her. I bet she was trying to scare him. Shocked at what she'd done, she dropped her weapon."

Matthews turned, "Okay, I'm done here, I'm heading down to the house. Anybody call her? Ron, have you tried to call her?" Reese didn't wait for an answer. He cut across the field and headed for the house.

Davis ran to catch up with Matthews. His duty belt and gear jostled with his weight and gait. "No sir, I didn't call—her cell phone was smashed in her kitchen."

"Anybody try her on the police radio?"

"No sir."

Matthews stopped, looked at the ground, then turned and continued on his path.

∽ ∽ ∽

Matthews walked into Kate's house like he owned the place, with Davis on his six. One technician was taking prints while another snapped photos. Matthews grabbed some evidence gloves and put them on. He ignored the footies for his boots.

"What do we think happened here?"

The technician taking photos looked away from his camera.

"Above my pay grade, sir. But if I were to guess, someone kicked in the back door. Whoever it was didn't have O'Dell's size thirteen boot."

"Was it a man's boot?"

"Hard to say."

Matthews voice got a little louder. "Are we investigating a kidnapping here?"

The officer looked up from dusting prints. "We've just started processing the scene. We've found one set of prints—probably Kate's. A couple of others unidentified, but I think they're women's prints."

Matthews left the officers in the kitchen, strode into the living room, and spotted the bathrobe on the floor. He surveyed the rest of the room: television, sofa, chair, table, light, kick bag. *No pictures.* He picked up the robe with his gloved hand. *No rips or tears.*

He moved into the bedroom and walked around the bed which was carefully made. "What do you think happened, Davis?"

Davis pointed at the techs. "Let's keep looking and keep our thoughts to ourselves for a moment. You lead."

Matthews opened the wardrobe and pointed. "These aren't Kate's clothes." He pulled a pink blouse off the rod and showed it to Davis.

Ron moved over closer, took the blouse from Matthews. "Size medium, could be."

"Look at this one, size large. Keep this to ourselves, Davis. And these aren't Kate's shoes."

Davis nodded.

The two moved into the bathroom, which was immaculate. There were only a couple of off-brand shampoos and soaps.

Matthews left the room and spoke in a hushed tone to Davis. "The lack of hair care products and make-up isn't fooling me. She deliberately left us a message. The good news is, she ran. She wasn't abducted." He continued, "I'm gonna try to reach her on the radio. You stay here and see if you can learn anything. I'm trusting you, Davis, like Kate trusted you. Don't share any info."

CHAPTER TWENTY-THREE

CONVENT, HERE I COME

K ate knew the route to the convent without having to check a map. She didn't have to think—all she had to do was drive. By heading west instead of north, she could listen to the police scanner for forty-five minutes and piece together what was happening at the crime scene.

The radio broke into her thoughts. "Contact 201, advise him to contact the sheriff by cell."

201, that's Reese's number. He'll know in a few minutes that O'Dell has been shot. He'll be worried about me.

❧   ❧   ❧

Kate strained to listen as she drove down a blacktop road, avoiding the main highway. She pulled over into a small roadside park, removed her camo pants and replaced her boots with ballerina flats. She looked in the rear-view mirror, applied pale pink lipstick, and powdered her face and eyebrows with light make-up. She replaced her watch with a smaller more feminine version, checked the time, and realized she'd been on the road for forty-three minutes.

Two more miles and I will officially let go of my old life.

"2-0-4. Check in! Over."

Kate's heart skipped a beat when she heard Reese's voice calling for her over the airwaves. *I could answer, he can't track me by radio signal.* Kate laughed at herself. *What would I say? "Hey, Reese. I'm on the run."*

"2-0-4, I know you can hear me. Check in. Over."

Kate's thoughts flew into overdrive. *Why am I running? I didn't shoot him, but how would I explain? Who did murder him? It was a cop—and all fingers will be pointing at me.*

Kate waited, hoping Reese would radio again.

"Kate, answer me. Or call me on my cell. Over."

Don't . . . I can't. I could be the next one murdered. How would I explain I have this car, the scene at my house? Drive. She reached over and turned off the police scanner. "Goodbye, Reese. Goodbye, Old Life."

She wiped a tear from her eye and looked at herself in the rearview mirror. *I'm no longer Kate Anderson. But who am I?*

❦   ❦   ❦

Kate arrived at the back door of the convent at two a.m. She grabbed her go-bag and a small flashlight, found the keypad to the back door to the little chapel and punched in the numbers 1-8-5-7, the year the chapel was built. The door popped open, and she slid through the opening into another world. A large cross hung on the wall as the centerpiece. Candles danced in front of a statue of the Virgin Mother. Small kneelers lined both sides of the aisle. A life-sized angel standing next to the

141

door startled Kate. He was holding a bowl of Holy Water. She dipped her fingers into the water and made the Sign of the Cross.

A shoe-sized, locked metal box with a slit in the top sat on a table next to the angel. As directed, she deposited her Missouri Driver's license, library cards, and finally her Probation and Parole ID through the slot. These would be used to make a fake ID for some other woman on the run.

Kate found the small sliding door which led to a closet-sized room with a single bed and reading light. Another sliding door led to a small bathroom with a sink and toilet.

She flopped onto the bed and was surprised how hard it felt. *Well, this isn't very comfy.* She patted the hard bed in disbelief, then removed her shoes. Wide awake, she dug in her bag, found a granola bar, and munched on it as she examined her new ID. Jane Jones was significantly heavier than Kate. Kate smiled wide and puffed up her cheeks and squinted her eyes. *I think I pass for Jane. J.J.—I like it. Weight Watchers worked wonders for people like me. Don't cry, Jane. We're not going to cry. Reese, where are you? Are you thinking of me?*

She flipped on the reading light and opened the book she'd packed, *Women Who Run with The Wolves* by Dr. Pinkola Estes.

I wonder if he's at my house. I'm three days late. I hope it's just stress. I wonder how long before I take a pregnancy test.

❦ ❦ ❦

"Wake up!" Sister Anne shook Kate's shoulders.

Kate sat up and rubbed her eyes. "That was the best sleep I've had in months, even though it's been just a few hours. What time is it?"

"It's already ten. I didn't wake you for prayers or breakfast, but we have to move you soon. You are one hot firecracker! Your picture is all over breaking news. They said you murdered Robert O'Dell. Did you shoot him, Kate? Stop, I don't want to know. We thought you were going to Des Moines last night."

Kate took the cup of steaming coffee from Sister Anne. "Thank you, Sister. This smells wonderful. I didn't know what to do. It's hard to explain, but there was a change in plans and Rosie told me . . . umm . . . if there was any change in plans, I should come here. I didn't leave as expected—and I thought coming here was the best thing. I knew the way."

"You're upset. It's fine, but it does complicate things. Don't tell me what happened. We're putting you in the back of a van this morning with five other sisters. I've brought you some plain clothes, a prayer book, and a pamphlet about what is expected of a novice. We're sending you to Kansas City. We don't think they will look for you amongst the inner-city poor. The sisters won't ask any questions—but the priests will. Nosy busy bodies. Avoid them. Just try to look plain. Cover most of your hair."

"Sister, wait! What if I get caught? I don't want to get you into trouble."

"You won't get caught. But if you do, ask for an attorney. Don't say anything until an attorney talks to you. Don't say anything about us, ever."

Kate looked at Sister Anne. "Please tell me something, anything. I need to talk."

Sister Anne sat next to Kate on the bed. "I know you have questions. Don't you see, it's best if you don't know anything?" She paused and looked at Kate. "You're so lost, aren't you? I have a few minutes, but you cannot share this with anyone. One night, sometime in the early eighties, a young woman showed up at the back door of the convent. It was storming, one of those nights when no one in their right mind would be out. To begin with, we thought the back door was banging. When I went to check, there was this poor creature, just a shadow against the lightning. She had been badly beaten by her husband and begged us not to turn her away. Back then, we had the retirement home and a good nurse on staff. After a few days, Brenda's story unfolded. It was obvious she couldn't go back to her old life. She'd left her husband several times, but he always found her.

Sister Anne shook her head, "It was awful. I've never seen someone beaten like that."

"Go on, what did you do?"

"I knew Sally from the small town I grew up in. She was a donor to the convent, so I had her information. She made transportation arrangements. I didn't ask questions and Sally didn't give any information. That's how we have always operated. It keeps everyone safe. Sally has done all the networking. We got a post card from Brenda months later, and then all correspondence dropped off. Sally said it was best. Since then, we got a few more women each year. Sally has sent a few our way. We don't know how the word gets out."

"I'm so thankful, but I can't be the one to jeopardize your operation. I'm afraid if I turn myself in, I'll be killed in jail."

"Don't worry about us. Stay to yourself; don't ask questions—that way, people are less likely to ask you questions. Stick to your cover story. Right now, you are a novice in training. Assume the role. Just pretend you're back in Catholic school."

"Sister, you have to tell me about the witches' party. It was weird."

"Oh, the girls were just having a little fun. It's the witchy time of year. They knew they had a male audience. They were also having a little fun with *you*. It was a play on words, 'coven—convent.' Kate, you're so gullible and young. The ladies were being silly, having a few laughs."

"Okay, I get it, I think.

"You have your burner phone?"

"Yes, with Rosie's number plugged in."

"This will blow over, but it may take a while. Keep your go-bag with you. It will seem awkward at first, but then it will be second nature."

"Sister, I didn't shoot him."

Sister Anne hugged Kate. "Praise the Lord. Do you know where you want to go?"

"I was in foster care for a short time after my parents were killed in a plane crash. I always thought I would visit that couple. I think this is my chance to do all those things I wanted to do. You know, like what would you do if you knew this was your last day of freedom?"

"Like a bucket list?"

"Yes, I think so. The last time I looked, they were in Georgia. They are probably retired and the last thing they need is a fugitive. But maybe I can help them in some way."

"I'll pass it on to Sally. Time to say goodbye. I'll pack you a sandwich. Change your clothes and come to the back door of the kitchen. Look and act like a nun: pray, and most importantly, don't get caught. I may not see you again. I pray for your safety and that the officers will find the real murderer soon."

"Sister, you have to tell Pops I'm safe."

"I'll make arrangements, Kate. Call Rosie when you're ready to move on."

CHAPTER TWENTY-FOUR

THE DEAL

Kingseat, Missouri

The three men stood on a sturdy dock which had been built by an Eagle Scout earning his badge. On the bank of the Grand River, the willows were turning shades of yellow, and the sun sifted through their leaves. The greens and gold accented the white on the bark of the birch and cottonwood trees. The three old friends were determined to enjoy the lazy afternoon. They studied their fishing poles as they sipped on bottles of Bud. Their histories linked them together like brothers.

The governor, Dan, spoke first. "Hell, Reese, you have to take the job. I'm running for re-election and the O'Dell family is making a big deal about the fact that the girl has not been apprehended. I've got some real competition in this campaign. I need to shut them up. You're a natural tracker. You always get your man and you'll find her." He paused before launching into his best pitch. "It's for her own good, while she still has connections. She's got a price on her head."

"Are you done?" Reese said. "I'm acutely aware she's got bounty hunters after her."

Cliff broke in. "I agree, Reese. I'll be moving up to the federal bench someday, so right now is the time, when I'm still the circuit judge. I can pull strings when she's apprehended. It's a no-brainer for her to come in now. We'll get her moved immediately to another jail and jurisdiction."

"Dan, don't you think if I could find her, I'd have already done it? Trust me, I've made it a twenty-hour-a-week job. It's like she vanished."

Cliff spoke again. "Think about it, Reese, taking a job with the marshal's office would give you a team. I know you have some leads. Her grandfather knows something. Take the job, it's a bump in pay, and you could spend your entire time looking for her."

Reese's bobber went under—he had snagged a big cat. His pole bent as he reeled. He stepped forward, moving toward the fish.

The judge stood up and peered into the water. "Don't lose him, don't let him get under the dock." Reese stepped back as the pole bent further into the water and dipped straight at the dock. "How am I supposed to stop him from going under there?"

"He's *under* the dock," the judge said.

Reese stepped back, and the catfish reared his head out of the water then flipped his tail. The pole snapped into two pieces. The top half made a little pirouette as if waving goodbye, then disappeared.

Reese laughed. "I'll be damned. I need a bigger pole."

Dan slapped Reese on the back, "How many times do I have to tell you, do *not* step back from the fish. This isn't calf roping."

Cliff laughed. "It's like he flipped you off at the end."

"Well, I reckon I'll never learn. That was a big one." The three sat down in their camp chairs, the excitement over for the day. The governor checked his watch and looked at the two highway patrolmen standing on the hill behind, guarding him. "It's time." He stood next to Reese.

Reese studied the governor. "You can really get me a job with the U.S. Marshal's office? You got that kind of juice?"

"Yeah, I got that kind of juice, but I'll lose it, if I lose this election. It's an embarrassment that I had that loser O'Dell on my security team to begin with. Slapping and stalking women, it's ridiculous. I'm still mad at you for not informing me."

"It was an ongoing investigation. We were trying to find missing women. If I remember correctly, finding the missing women was a priority for your administration?"

The two stared at each other as if squaring off for a fight.

Cliff jumped up and stepped between the two men. He held up his hands like stop signs directed at them. "Back off, both of you. Fighting like children won't solve a thing. Reese, sit down."

Reese sat down on a bench. "Don't you think I've kicked myself enough for not handling things differently? Where will I be working out of? I can't live in the city."

"We'll get you an office in North Kansas City, near the airport. I'd recommend you live in Platte City. You'll be doing some flying."

"I want to take an officer with me. He's top notch. A computer whiz and a chess player. He can see a strategy I can't."

"Any more demands?"

"Cliff, can you make sure she is transferred out of the Kingseat jail, and that bail is set?"

"You find the safest jail and I'll get her transferred there."

"I don't want her in the 'safest jail.' I want her bonded out."

"Yes, I'll get a low bond set. Tell her grandfather to post his house as collateral—she won't jump bail with him having his house on the line."

"I'll need a job when this is done. I'm not a marshal. I don't want to spend my life on the road. Get me a signed offer with a good expense account. In the meantime, I'll talk to the grandfather."

    ∾ ∾ ∾

Matthews sat in the office inside his duplex apartment. It had not changed much since Kate had driven into his garage. The only addition was the white murder board which held pictures, dates, and timelines. O'Dell, in his deputy uniform. O'Dell and snapshots with his biker friends. The suspect side of the board contained two pictures, O'Dell's uncle, the sheriff of Chariton County, and Marcus Lucas, the head of the biker gang. Kate's picture had been moved to the back side of the board.

Matthews pulled the picture of the sheriff off the board and mumbled to himself. "Why would you want your cousin dead? Political reasons, family reasons, moral reasons? You have means, motive, and opportunity." He pinned the photo back on the board, then stepped toward the photo of Marcus Lucas. "How 'bout you, Marcus, why would *you* want O'Dell dead? Money, power, women? It's always money, power, women. Where were *you* the night O'Dell was murdered?"

He looked again at the crime scene photo. "Double-tapped like a cop. Or an execution by a biker gang. Which was it?"

He moved the board so he could look at the back side of it. Kate's picture hung in the middle. He had a timeline to trace her movements the night of the murder. There were pictures of Kate's cottage, her car, her duty weapon. There were also pictures of a blue Mazda passing through a check point on Highway 36— headed west. He concentrated on the photos of Dirty Sally's Bar, Sally O'Malley, snapshots of the little cabin out back, and of Sic'em.

He scowled. "Kate, where'd ya get the car? Why would you be headed west? Sally, why do you keep lying to me?" *There are leads. The trail is cold, but she didn't just disappear.*

Matthews looked at the contract sent over by the U.S. Marshal's Service and scrawled his signature in the line provided. "Best of all, I'll demand that Sheriff O'Dell hand over the victim's file."

∽ ∽ ∽

Governor Dan Hand held a press conference on the courthouse steps in Kingseat. A small crowd of news reporters and a crew from a television station with cameras were gathered in front of him. The reporters snapped pictures as the news camera zoomed in on the governor and Matthews, who stood beside him. "The murder investigation of Robert O'Dell has been handed over to the U.S. marshal's office. Reese Matthews has been appointed the lead investigator in the federal apprehension of Kate Anderson."

He paused for dramatic effect and said, "We cannot have someone suspected of the cold-blooded killing of a Missouri deputy sheriff not face the consequences of the crime. The Missouri task force does not have enough resources to handle the case, so we're bumping it up to the feds."

A loud reporter interrupted the governor. "Is Kate Anderson still the prime suspect in this case?"

The governor said, "Obviously, she's innocent until proven guilty. If anyone knows the whereabouts of Kate Anderson, please contact the task force. There are deputies handing out business cards with the telephone number. That is all for this morning. After lunch, we will tour the new city solar farm."

Dared to Run

As Matthews walked down the steps behind the governor, reporters surrounded him. One news podcaster dressed in a t-shirt and jeans shouted, "What leads do you have in finding the suspect?," while a reporter from a news station stuck a microphone in his face. "Tell me about your team."

He muttered, "No comment." He made his way to his SUV and swung into the Jeep. As he started to shut the door, a withered hand stopped him.

"How could you do this?" The man spoke above a whisper. "How could you take this job to track her down? She trusted you—you were her friend."

Another reporter shoved a microphone in the old man's face. "Are you Mr. Anderson?" Without waiting for a reply, the reporter continued, "Mr. Anderson, do you think your granddaughter killed Robert O'Dell?"

"Of course she killed him! I didn't raise that girl to be slapped around by a man."

Matthews exited the SUV and yelled at the reporters as they snapped photos of the two men. "Enough, now. Let Mr. Anderson go home. I'll give you a statement but leave him alone." He shouted to a deputy. "Get some crowd control over here. Mr. Anderson, let me take you home."

"Leave me alone, I have my car." Anderson walked away, shooing the reporters as if they were flies. Two deputies ran to catch up with him, as he walked faster than they anticipated.

Reese called the reporters over to him as a diversion and fielded a few questions about his newly formed

153

team. As soon as the old man was in his car, Matthews walked away.

CHAPTER TWENTY-FIVE

BLACK ANGEL

R osie Martin bounced in her big rig, carrying a load to Kansas City, Missouri. She sang along with country western songs and smiled to herself. She had an almost-pitch-perfect voice and could have been a star, if stage fright and a bad man had not gotten in the way. After a while, her mood turned somber and she shut off the radio, musing about the passenger she would soon pick up and take to Des Moines. Kate Anderson was one of Rosie's favorite people.

After Kate's parents had died, Rosie had appointed herself Kate's real-life guardian angel. At first, it was making sure the girl got home from school. Her grandparents barely noticed the orphan who resided with them.

Then, Kate was bullied after school. Rosie waited for the three boys to leave one day and followed them to a park. All she had to do was crack her bullwhip to make the boys snivel, cry, and promise not to pick on girls.

Rosie's thoughts turned to the obscene phone caller who had stalked Kate in high school. *I turned into a black angel that night. I didn't really mean to kill that young man. He shouldn't have eaten all those false morel mushrooms. I*

155

just wanted to make him sick . . . Lord forgive me. The Third Street exit loomed ahead, and Rosie cursed as she missed her turn. She was traveling on Interstate 35 going south, with a quick stop planned in the market district. She turned on the Fifth Street exit and when she saw a sign for the Arabia Steamboat Museum, she pulled behind The Corner restaurant and backed the truck to the loading dock.

A tall bearded man in his mid-forties pounded on the side of the tractor-trailer door. Rosie cranked her window down. "Hey, Hank. How's it going tonight?"

"Hey, Rosie, we thought we were going to see you next week. What's the rush?"

"Dispatch shoved my schedule around. Some emergency cargo I'm supposed to pick up, but not until I unload this soon-to-be-expired beer."

"My crew's all lined up. It won't take long. You want to go in and have a meal?"

"No, thanks, I better get on the road. I'll just sit here and let you guys unload, if you don't mind."

"Okay, Rose, suit yourself. We'll send you a check at the end of the month."

"Sounds good, thanks."

Rosie watched in her side mirror as the men unloaded the truck. Her heart raced as she anticipated Kate's arrival. When the unloading was done, she began to pull away from the dock, and as planned, Kate rapped on the passenger side of the truck. Rosie slowed to a full stop and the young woman, dressed in a green stocking hat, black jacket and pants, opened the door and crawled inside.

Kate beamed from ear to ear as she climbed into her seat. "Hey Rosie, thanks for the lift!"

"Get, in, get in. It's cold out there. How you doin', Kate—I mean, Jane?"

Kate plopped into the seat, threw her backpack on the floor, and searched for the seat belt. "I'm great, Rosie, I'm so glad I'm no longer a novice in the convent. Wow, that's a lot of praying."

"The world needs prayers."

"I guess. I really think there are better ways to spend one's time."

"You ready for your new life in Georgia?"

"I'm super ready. And thank you, Rosie. I know this would ruin your life if we got caught. You'd sit in jail and probably lose your trucker's license."

"My story is I picked up a hitch-hiker, and as far as anybody knows I haven't seen you since you were a kid. But the truth is, I've been looking after you like you were my own little sister since you were five. I don't take these kinds of risks for everyone. None of the network does. This was an extraordinary circumstance."

"You've been watching over me?"

"Sure, Kate. Your granddad saved my family, so that made him family to me. We're kin—not the blood kind. Never mind that. We have only a few hours. I brought you some gifts and some grub. You want to dig in that bag?"

"Wow, thanks." Kate unzipped the bag which was wedged in the space between the two seats. "It looks like cherry pie. Yum."

She laid the pie on her lap and pulled a month's worth of local newspapers out of the bag.

"Oh, what a gift. I'm a little homesick. Who knows me this well?"

"Those are from me. I knew you would love them. One of them has a great picture of your grandad and Reese Matthews on the front steps of the courthouse. Did you hear Matthews took over the investigation?"

"Yes, I saw it on the news. Poor Pops."

Rosie laughed and downshifted for traffic. "Your grandad hasn't had this much excitement in years. It probably takes his mind off Grandma Helen."

"How's she doing?"

"She's recovering from her hip surgery, but she's not well. Smoking all those years is taking its toll." She paused. "In the bag, there's also your waitress uniform, some shoes and boots, a pair of glasses with clear lenses and some cash from Pops. Oh, and two drop phones. My number is already plugged into them. You'll leave yours with me and we'll move it on to someone else."

"Thanks, Rosie. I'll check this all out later. I'm going to eat my pie. Where are we heading?"

"I've got a load to pick up in Des Moines, and then I have to head north. We've arranged for a vehicle for you. It looks like a clunker, but it runs good. Unless you've changed your mind about going to Georgia and want to go north with me."

"No, no. Georgia here I come. It'll be a great time to be south."

"You'll find a map and a suggested route. There'll be one safe house on the way. Just take your time, don't speed, and don't wig out if you see cops. Keep your hair covered and maybe add the glasses. Avoid cameras—the big truck stops all have them. Head for the small gas stations. Travel at night. Stay at the cheap hotels."

"Gotcha. But, if I were to go north with you, what would the route look like?"

"We've got a safe house in Lincoln, Nebraska. There's a vet there that always needs help with his dog kennel. You'd stay a couple weeks, then north to North Dakota. We have an eccentric woman and you'd fit right in as her niece. You'd probably stay a few days until we could place you in Canada. We've got lots of places in Canada. It's a big place, plus they're not looking for fugitives from America—especially females. We've also got a place in DC. Interesting enough, there's a federal judge there that has a basement apartment."

"Oh, I'd love to see DC. It's on my list."

"Georgia, then DC, how's that sound? I don't know how long you'll be able to stay in DC—lots of cameras—but maybe if you dressed like a dude, you could stay six weeks or so and be safe."

Rosie concentrated on the road, while Kate dug into her bag for a battery-operated reading light. "Will it bother you if I look at these papers? What a fun gift for me."

"No, it won't bother me, unless you shine the light in my eyes. I laid one out for you on top. Some kid named Art Gage won ten grand in the Country Club tournament by shooting a hole in one. He'd just turned eighteen."

Kate flipped to the sports page. "Wow, what a great pic—and birthday present. Art Gage, I'll have to try to run into you someday. Maybe your luck will run off on me."

CHAPTER TWENTY-SIX

RUN, RUN, RUN AWAY

Rebel, Georgia, eleven months later

K ate bent over the table, wiping it vigorously. It appeared from the viewpoint of two of the men sitting at the table that her cleavage was doing most of the work, a technique she'd perfected at this restaurant. She was sure this skill made her employable at most small restaurants in America.

Her mission today: observe the black sedan parked across the street. The restaurant faced south, its front window a vignette featuring an old stove, pots, pans, and dishes, all carefully marked for sale. The pictures on the wall featured area artists, and the different flavors of jelly on the tables were made by all local jammers. Everything was for sale. Not one inch of the restaurant held wasted space.

Two of the old men sitting at the table stared down the front of her uniform, while the other two stared at her wiggling back side. She glanced at the clock on the wall, slightly easing her cleavage a little closer to Richard, one of the four regulars. *The cops have been out there an hour.*

She stood up and playfully pulled the cap off of Bruce, another of the four. She stuck it sideways on her head and peeked out the window.

"Why are you so obsessed with this table? This is the fourth time you've wiped it in an hour—not that I mind the view," quipped the old marine.

"What's wrong with you, old man? I believe you're lookin' a little too close at my ass."

The group laughed and one of the men slapped his knee, laughing.

"You tryin' to get a tip out of Ole' Toad here? You know he's leavin' you a quarter no matter what you do."

Kate looked at the four old men. *I'm going to miss them.* She replaced the hat on Bruce's head and smiled sweetly at Toad. "I guess I'll take my leave, if I'm not going to get any tips. You know where the coffee pot is."

She twirled her rag round and round as she departed, singing an old hymn, then untied her apron and called out to the owner of the café, "Clyde, I've got everything ready for the lunch crowd, I'm running over to check on my truck at Jerry's."

There was no need for Clyde to answer. Kate was gone.

❧   ❧   ❧

Richard Mullen, a retired Marine, knew everything that went on in the town. Unlike many men his age—seventy-five—he had lost none of his six foot two inches in height. He worked out at the gym three times a week, cleared fence rows, and drove tractors with men a couple of decades younger. His appearance was changing, though—once a handsome man with an eager face and bright lights in his eyes, he now looked more like a wise old owl.

Richard had a reserved seat facing the door. Anyone trying to take his seat was waved out with his cane. He noticed a black sedan and saw men snapping pictures. He sighed. *I wonder where she'll head. I'll probably never see her again.* He wanted to follow her out. He wanted one last look at the cheery waitress who brightened his day and breathed life into this restaurant and this small southern town.

Richard had been around the world. He knew when pieces didn't fit—and that girl stoppin' and stayin' in this town—didn't fit. Now he knew why. Cops were after her. He wanted to buy her time, so he didn't head out to his red Ford pickup. As soon as the cops exited the car, he started his slow rise from the booth, all six foot two of him, his height blocking the view of the young woman leaving out the back door. He was determined to give her a few extra minutes.

Two men wearing blue suitcoats, tan pants, and sunglasses came into the restaurant, sat in a booth, and glanced at their menus.

The man who looked like his nickname, Toad, said to Richard, "Are ya goin' or are ya stayin'?"

"I'm obviously stayin'."

The two new men looked up from their menus.

163

"You might want to wait on your new customers, Clyde," Richard said, chuckling.

Clyde looked up from the potato he was peeling. "Where in the hell's Jane?"

The two men sprung to their feet and took a few steps toward the back of the café, only to be blocked by a senior citizen who danced side to side in front of them with his cane. One of the men jumped into a booth and over the back of it to avoid the old man.

"It looks like the excitement's over boys, I think I'll go on home," said Richard.

He ambled out to his truck, carrying the heavy weight of his loss with him. When he reached the pickup, he struggled to get in, leaned over, and started the engine. Patsy Cline sang on the radio. He touched his front pocket and pulled out the note she'd left him, written in perfect penmanship.

Dear Richard:

As soon as possible, please tell Clyde and Lulu I love them. Thank them for everything they have done for me. I know this is not the life they hoped for me, but my life is full. I'm living my dream. If I hadn't been accused of murder, I might not have had the chance to really live.

LuLu, Clyde, I'm the little girl, Kate, you took care of after my parents' plane crashed nearly twenty-two years ago.

Richard, you old coot, I guess you're all right too. Don't forget me.

Love, Kate (aka Jane)

P.S. I loved your stories, maybe you'll be in my novel someday.

Richard put the note back in his pocket and patted it. Tears formed in his eyes. He wiped them away with the back of his liver-spotted hand.

I won't forget you, Girlie. Godspeed.

CHAPTER TWENTY-SEVEN

FINDING JANE

Rebel, Georgia

Steve Blakely and his partner, Ralph Dorney, returned to the diner carrying a black bag of gear. Blakely, the agent Matthews brought from Probation and Parole, was assigned as lead investigator. The chase out the back door into the alley had been a waste. Kate Anderson had just disappeared—again. She could have gone in any direction, into any building, down alleyways, into bars and shops. What they needed was a positive ID.

Dorney spoke on the phone with Reese Matthews, the chief investigator for the apprehension unit. "Yes, sir, we think it was Kate. No sir, no good pictures. The fact she ran . . . "

Blakely had ascertained the diner was owned by Clyde and Lulu Harrison. At Blakely's request, Clyde had called his wife at the local salon, and she was on her way back. Word had already spread around town, and people were gawking from across the street. Blakely saw a short, plump woman, dressed in pink, swinging her purse as she walked down the street. It swung like a metronome. Her blonde coifed hair did not move as she stepped along. She turned like a raging bull when she came to the front door of the café.

Blakely opened the door.

"Thank you, young man," Lulu said.

"Yes ma'am," Blakely said, "I'm sorry for the interruption in your hair appointment."

Lulu glared at him.

Blakely stammered. "Sorry, ma'am, we need to ask you some questions."

Lulu flipped the sign on the door to read CLOSED. "Clyde, where are you hiding?"

She turned, marched to a front table, then took a deep breath and a seat. Clyde came out of the kitchen to join her. "Grab the coffee pot, Clyde."

He removed his white apron which was smudged with sausage gravy from the breakfast crowd. He brought the pot and poured coffee into white mugs. Blakely sat down. He held out a picture of a young woman and showed it to Lulu. "Do you know this woman?"

Lulu took the picture, looked at it and passed it to Clyde, who waved it away, got up slowly, and walked back into the kitchen.

"Look what you've gone and done. You've upset Clyde."

"Yes, ma'am. I see that. Why's he so upset? Is this woman your waitress?"

"Listen to me young man, you come in here, take over our restaurant, call me from the hairdresser . . . " Lulu stopped. "Kate Anderson?"

167

"Yes, ma'am, Kate Anderson, from Kingseat, Missouri. She's twenty-six, why?"

"Clyde, did you hear that?"

"I'm calling our attorney."

Blakely followed him into the kitchen. "Sir, we don't think you've done anything wrong. If you could just answer some questions, we'll be gone."

Clyde returned to the table and looked at his wife. He picked up her hand and kissed it.

"Do you know this woman?" Blakeley handed the picture to Clyde.

"Maybe, maybe not. That might be our waitress, Jane. She left a little before you two fellas came in here."

Lulu picked up on Clyde's cue—talk and stall. "I left at about nine-forty-five, didn't I, Clyde? You see, I get my hair done once a week over at the 'Clip and Snip.' Marcie has done my hair for the past twenty years. People say I look like Betty White—don't you think I look like Betty White?"

"Sir, when was the last time you saw her?"

"Who?" Clyde asked.

"Your waitress."

"Oh her . . . oh, I don't know. Like I said, she left right before you came in. She should've been back by now. I wonder what's keepin' her."

❧   ❧   ❧

A helicopter hovered and landed in a field near the restaurant. The townspeople in the area gawked as Reese Matthews stepped out and headed to the café.

Those inside the café saw a tall shadow walk by the window and swing the door open. "Dorney, get over to the garage and find out about the car," Matthews ordered. "Get with the local enforcement officers. We need to find that vehicle. Blakely and I will handle this."

Matthews removed his white Stetson and blue suit coat and hung them on a rack by the door. He slowly unbuttoned his starched white shirt sleeves and rolled them up twice. He pulled out a chair and took a seat at the table. "Mornin', ma'am, sir, how're ya doing this morning? A little sad and confused? You got any pie, coffee? The agency will pay you for your closed time—reimburse you for everything."

Blakely looked at his boss. *I can't believe his mood.* He mirrored Reese by getting up and hanging up his jacket, but he left his cuffs untouched and buttoned at the wrist.

Clyde struggled to get up. "I'll go make a fresh pot of coffee. Jane—I mean our waitress—baked some fresh pie this morning." He disappeared into the kitchen.

"Ma'am, my name's Reese Matthews. I'm gonna level with you. I've been tracking Kate Anderson for about thirteen months now. She worked for me at Probation and Parole in Missouri. She's a fine woman and a great investigator. I pulled some strings to get this assignment about four months ago. 'Why?' you might ask, and I'll tell you why—I'm trying to save her life. She's accused of killing a deputy sheriff. As, you can imagine, with a charge like that—murdering a deputy sheriff in cold blood . . . "

Lulu gasped and put her hand over her mouth. "I just can't believe it could be our Jane."

"Jane, did you say? What's her last name?"

Lulu looked at him. "Jane, that's what we called her."

"She worked here nine or ten months, and you don't know her last name?"

Lulu said, "She was a contractor. She worked for room and board and tips and we paid her for her pies. We don't know anyone wanted for murder of a deputy—especially from Missouri. Half of them are Yankees, anyway."

Clyde came out of the kitchen. "Looks like we've got cherry, apple crumb. Which piece would you like, Officer Matthews?"

"I'll take a slice of that cherry. What would you like, Blakely?" He put his hand on Blakely's shoulder and stood up. "Let me get the coffee pot. Clyde, have a seat. I'll help myself. You keep a running tab, all right, Clyde?"

Matthews walked into the kitchen and spoke through the pass-through window into the front dining area. "You've got a mighty clean kitchen in here, folks. Looks like Jane made *several* pies. Is this normal or was she expecting us?" He didn't wait for an answer. "Blakely, why don't you come in and take some pictures—then we can cut a piece to eat." Matthews opened the refrigerator, "It looks like there's banana, too, or Clyde—is that *your* favorite?"

Blakely rounded into the kitchen and took pictures. Matthews muttered softly, "Scan them for prints."

"Yes, sir."

Lulu hit Clyde. "You hoggin' that banana pie, old man?" She got up and bustled into the kitchen. "You're mighty charmin' aren't you, Officer? Or is it Chief Matthews—can I call you 'Chief?' Good lookin' man like yourself, nice and easy and friendly, you think you can charm your way into our kitchen, and we'll spill our guts because *we're* old and *you're* mighty fine?"

"Well, ma'am." He drawled the "ma'am," trying to mimic the style of rural Georgia. "Thank you for the compliment. Not my usual style, as you can imagine. I bark orders and interrogate people. She's gone, and we're not going to find her hiding under a bed. Whatever you tell me now is background information. I'm telling you the truth." Matthews looked into Lulu's eyes. "I'm trying to save her life. Some trigger-happy deputy is going to shoot her and get a medal for doing it."

Lulu matched his stare. Reese returned it with his best sincere look. *About fourteen months ago Kate brought me a pie. She loved pie.* "Who *doesn't* like a piece of pie?"

"Well, before you tear up my kitchen and bring a forensics team in here lookin' for evidence, I'm gonna cooperate with you. But, you're not gonna find any fingerprints, so don't be inkin' up the place. And—just in case she needs a little more time—I'm gonna show you our southern hospitality by cutting you a piece of our favorite dessert. We're gonna sit down and enjoy it, because it's all we have left of her. I don't imagine we'll be seeing that girl for a long time."

"It's a deal." Matthews shook Lulu's hand. The two returned to the table. "But this isn't a crime scene and we've got scanners for fingerprints now."

Blakely remained in the kitchen, scanned for prints, and looked for evidence.

After a few minutes, Matthews said, "That's about the tastiest cherry pie I've ever had."

Lulu leaned back and said, "Ask your questions."

"Well, ma'am, I'm going to get right to the point. What kind of vehicle does she drive?"

Clyde said, "Truth is, I don't know. I think it was a blue Chevy pickup, but it could've been a Ford. I didn't ever see her drive it. It was vintage. Jerry was restoring it."

Blakely came from the kitchen with a small electronic device. "Nothing sir, it's been wiped down. I think we have a few sets of a man's prints, but that's it."

Matthews held up the picture. "Can you give me a positive ID? Is this your waitress, Jane?"

Lulu took the picture and looked at it. "I'm not really sure. And, that's the truth. Our Jane was younger than the woman in the picture. Your woman looks unhappy and stressed. Our Jane was the sweetest girl. Do you have any more pictures of your Kate Anderson? Maybe when she was younger?"

CHAPTER TWENTY-EIGHT

ACADEMY AWARD

C hase Baxter had dreamed of being an actor from the time he was four years old. He had used his college money to leave home and fly out to LA, hoping to be discovered. Chase loved the big city and had no intention of returning to Rebel, Georgia. But life has a way of changing plans. When his father was killed in an accident, Chase inherited the gas station and the debt. He returned home and now, three years later, he couldn't imagine any other life.

He sat in his organized office and pulled out two thousand dollars from his shirt pocket. He knew the deal on the pickup was too good to be true. *I can easily turn this into five—maybe more. Nah, I should keep the truck. It's a beauty.* He loved the blue color and the cream interior. He loved it, because his father once owned a similar truck, and Chase had rebuilt this one himself.

Why would Jane sell it? Why did she want it kept up on the rack until five o'clock as part of the deal? As he pondered his windfall, she knocked on the door.

Chase smiled and stood up. "Hiya, Jane."

"Hi, Chase. How's your mom? Did you get that First Alert System I suggested?"

"You were right—she resisted, but she loves it now. She keeps testing it—she doesn't believe the operator will really answer her."

"Oh my, honey, that's too funny. You're a good son, Chase. Listen, I've got to run. Is the truck up on the rack?"

"Yes ma'am. Listen, Miss Jane, I can't take advantage of you like this. Do you know what this truck is worth?"

"Do it for me, Chase, you'll be helping me. I know she's found a great home. I need the cash—you know how it is."

He handed her the money. Jane gave him the title in a white envelope. "It's legal, I promise. Please remember, leave the truck on the rack until five o'clock, okay?"

"Yes, ma'am, it's not moving till five o'clock."

"Can I get the key to the ladies' room?"

"It's open."

Kate walked toward the restroom, but turned, "Chase, Lulu hired a cute redhead over at the diner. I think she might like a ride in your new pickup."

The ding-ding of a car wanting service caught his attention, and Chase jogged out to greet his customer.

◈   ◈   ◈

Once in the restroom, Jane didn't hesitate as she pulled her ponytail straight up and cut it off above the rubber band. She looked in the mirror and saw a perfect bowl cut. She took the blonde five-minute hair dye, skimmed it through her short hair, and slicked it

174

straight back. She washed her face and smudged it with a little grease from the shop wall. *I hope I'm not bald when I stop in three hours.* Jane slid out of her waitress uniform and into her biker leather. She crammed the trash and the scissors inside her jacket pocket and looked at her waitress uniform. *Leave it.* It swung on the hook as she closed the door.

❧ ❧ ❧

Jane sped down the highway on her root-beer-colored 350 Harley. She loved the bike. Even though her mind should have been on questions like "are they following me?", "will they catch me?", "will I make my first stop tonight?", her first thought was *"Wow, these minimizer bras really work."* At the first mile marker, Jane reached into her jacket and released the ponytail. It flew for a second, then crashed onto the highway. She watched in her side mirror as an eighteen-wheeler ran over it. *There goes my old life in a million little pieces. Will I like my life now, pretending to be a dude?*

❧ ❧ ❧

Chase caught a glimpse of a figure coming out of the restroom dressed in black leather chaps and jacket. The jacket had a pit bull emblem on the back. *What the hell?* The figure ran around the corner, and he heard the distinctive sound of a Harley-Davidson starting up.

He began to whistle, because he knew his acting skills would be put to a test today.

Shortly after the Harley took off, Baxter heard a helicopter circling. He stepped outside the garage to watch a U.S. marshal's helicopter land in the nearby school lot. A burly, athletic man in a marshal's uniform exited the helicopter, ducking as he ran, then straightening up to a height of more than six feet. Chase watched the marshal head straight for the diner. He looked up at the pickup on his rack. His heart started to race.

❧ ❧ ❧

Chase was still whistling when a man who could have been a movie star playing the role of a U.S. marshal entered the garage. He was "tall, dark and handsome" as people in the entertainment biz might say. He ignored the man and whistled while he pried a tire off its rim. *You're just a stupid wise-cracking garage attendant—act like it. Should be a breeze.*

"I'm U.S. Marshal Dorney, I need to ask you a few questions." He flashed his badge.

Baxter wiped his hand on a rag and smiled. "I don't think you want to shake this hand, but nice to meet you, Marshal. What can I do for ya?"

The marshal held up a picture of Kate Anderson. "Do you know this woman?"

"I'm not sure. You been over to the café? It looks a bit like our waitress over there. Can't say for sure. They might be kin. Is that woman a cop? She looks like a cop."

"Sir, look closely, can you identify this woman?"

176

Chase squinted at the picture. "Nope, definitely not our Jane. Looks like her, though. What's she done?"

"She's wanted in connection with the murder of a deputy sheriff in Missouri."

"Holy shit." Chase continued to wipe his hands. "She come in here today?"

"Who? That woman? Nah."

The officer moved closer to the attendant. "The waitress from the café. Did she come in here today?"

"You just missed her. Wanted the bathroom."

"Did you see her leave?"

"Uhh, Jane? Well, no, I didn't see her leave."

"What was she wearing?"

"Excuse me?" The attendant scratched his head.

"We're trying to find a wanted fugitive. What was Jane wearing today?"

"I think she came in wearing her waitress uniform, can't say for sure. I'm not in the habit of checking out women and their clothes."

"Mr. Baxter, I'm sure my boss will need to speak to you. But first, I need to search your restroom."

"Knock yourself out, Boss. Door's open—"

Chase shouted. "Hey, Marshal, don't worry, I won't be checking you out when you leave the restroom." He threw his head back and chuckled. "What was she wearing? Wait till the guys hear *this* story."

At five o'clock, Baxter lowered the pickup from the rack. He looked in the window and noticed how spotless Jane kept the truck. Just for fun, he opened the driver's door and sat in the truck. He knew it would leave a huge smudge. He ran his hands around the steering wheel, touched the radio knobs, reached over and locked and re-locked the doors. He touched almost every surface. *That should take care of fingerprints. I should lock up, deal with this tomorrow.*

Blakely walked around the corner to Baxter's Garage. As he entered the building, there sat the truck they had been looking for all day. Every law enforcement agent in the state had a picture of this truck in their wanted poster information.

Blakely turned red in anger, and seeing Baxter sitting at his office desk, jogged over and barged through the door. "Damn it. Where is she? You're in quite a bit of trouble—lying to federal agents."

"I didn't lie." Chase looked at the agent acting braver than he felt. "Do I need an attorney?"

"Why didn't you tell us you had her truck?"

"That first guy didn't ask. He was just lookin' for this woman and wanted to know what Jane was wearin'. He was kinda in a hurry. You wanna look at the truck, it's clean, nothing in it."

Chase got up from the chair, led the investigator to the truck, unlocked it, and opened the door. "Clean as a whistle. Well, a few smudges from me."

"We're gonna need to bring a team over to go through it."

"Sure, sure, go ahead."

Blakely put on a pair of plastic gloves and opened the door, then the glove box.

"There's no paperwork in the glove box."

"No, I have it in the office. Jane was kinda naïve, I mean, she sold me this beautiful truck for two thousand dollars." Chase grinned at the officer. "Best deal I've made this year."

Blakely shook his head. "You can't possibly be this dumb. We're lookin' for a fugitive, and it doesn't enter your mind to tell us you've bought her truck?"

"Well believe it. Like I said, he didn't ask. I'm runnin' a garage, trying to stay afloat like most of the people in this town. Never had any dealings with cops before. Ya wanna see the paperwork? She titled it straight to my mom. I don't know how. I don't even have to do any paperwork. It's licensed and registered to my mother."

The two entered the office, and Chase handed him the title and registration papers. "She said it was legal. I don't know. Looks legit to me. She hardly ever drove it. It was in the shop getting restored most of the time."

Blakely studied the paperwork.

Chase said, "I'm as confused as you are. It's almost like—well, Agent, like she purchased the truck and drove the truck, just so you would look for her in the truck. Women, who can figure them out?"

Blakely brought out a small photo array of pictures of Kate Anderson. "Look at these pictures, can you identify this woman? Is *this* the woman that sold you the pickup?"

"No, sorry. I'm not sure."

179

"Drop the act. You know we can jam you up? We can close your shop, go through all your records."

Baxter stood up straight. "Knock yourself out. She's not here and I don't know anything. If I did know something—I sure as hell wouldn't tell you."

CHAPTER TWENTY-NINE

MEMORIES

T he group sat in the café and drank coffee. Matthews and Blakely chatted with Lulu and Clyde about all the items for sale. "All Jane's idea," Lulu told them. It was as if the coffee, the pie and Matthews' easy charm and manner had relaxed them— or as if the two marshals were simply two more customers and not law enforcement.

Lulu said, "She needed a room, so she went upstairs to the attic and brought down antique pieces, cleaned them up, and placed price tags on them."

Clyde said, "I told her, nobody's gonna buy that shit—I was wrong."

Lulu laughed. "She made herself a little apartment upstairs. After it was done, Clyde wanted to charge her rent. We made a thousand dollars the first month—on junk."

Matthews grinned. "Tell me about the first time you saw her."

Lulu looked at Clyde. "We've done the best we can for her. Maybe he's right, maybe he *will* save her life."

Clyde pointed at the door. "She came in here about nine or ten months ago, dressed in one of those little white waitress uniforms, and said she was looking for a job."

"She had sensible shoes on," Lulu said. "A pair just like these." She pointed at her feet, "Oh my goodness, how they've helped my feet and back. Jane bought these somewhere off the internet. I don't like it when girls come in here applying for a job with those flip-floppy shoes on—or high heels. How dumb are they? How they gonna work in shoes like that?"

"Lulu was against hiring her though, weren't you, Lulu?"

"Yes, what's a girl—a woman like that—doin' in a place like this? She didn't *look* like a waitress. Sure, she had a waitress uniform on, but I don't know, somehow she carried herself like she was a dancer or somethin'."

"I was won over with her smile and her little uniform," Clyde said.

Lulu slapped him on the arm. "Clyde, don't be indecent."

Matthews held up the photo of Kate. "So, folks, picturing her back then, did she resemble this photo?"

Clyde said, "Can't you see, we don't know. I know what you want to hear, but we just don't know."

"Did she give you a resume? Did she say where she was from?"

Lulu said, "Nah, she never spoke about her past. We didn't pry."

"You pried, you pried with a crowbar." Clyde threw his hands in the air and laughed. "Didn't pry."

"I think maybe that first day, she said she was from Kentucky. She had class. You could tell right off, she'd had a good upbringing. I knew she wasn't from Kentucky. Her accent was a little off, but I never could figure what was off about it—then decided it was just that she wasn't a local girl and had been to a good school."

"How old a gal was she?"

Clyde said, "I don't know, she was pretty young, maybe early twenties. I'm not much good about telling young women's ages. It's real hard when you get to be our age. I liked her right off. She always had ideas to make the place better, so we forgot that we were curious about her. She said she just stopped in here on her way to Florida. Isn't that what she said, Lulu?"

Lulu put down her cup. "She just fit in, like we'd known her forever. She went upstairs, cleaned the place, found herself an old single bed, bought a mattress, somehow cleaned and washed windows. Like I said, everything came from that old room upstairs. She found a woman to bring us fresh eggs every morning. Pretty soon we had fresh *vegetables* delivered, then *meat*, right to the back door. The food was fresher. The work was easier. Word started getting 'round—our business picked up. She bartered with some church women to make bread. People started coming into the restaurant just to see what we were havin'."

"Now hold on, Lulu, I remember now, I didn't hire her right off. When I turned her down, she asked if I might know of any other place that was hiring. I was worried my regular customers would go down the street."

"And that's when she started buttering *me* up—just like you, Chief Matthews. I don't take to people, don't trust' em, unless I know 'em. She introduced herself to me and asked if she could get me a cup of coffee and didn't I want to sit down? Jane told me she would work for tips the next two days, as a trial period. At the end of the second day, she was cleaning out upstairs. Do y'all get trainin' in cozying up to people? You *do*, don't ya?"

Chief Matthews interrupted, "So, you *do* think she was my investigator?"

Clyde answered, "Yes, that's right—*you* hired her. Anyways, back to the story. We started making more payments on the building, and instead of losing the place, we paid it off. We had a nice little party last week."

Lulu said, "Jane arranged it all. She got some picnic tables from the park, put up some lights. Clyde started drawing social security last week." Lulu's voice cracked. "She told us that night we might take a vacation and go see her down in Florida. She was preparing us, Clyde. It was her going away party."

"We won't be seeing her in Florida, will we, Chief?"

"She had an apartment upstairs?"

"Yes," Clyde said.

Blakely scooted his chair back. Chief Matthews stopped him.

"She's gone, isn't she? We're not going to see her again, are we?" Lulu started to cry. "We loved that girl so much. She turned this old restaurant around, and us, too. She gave us hope. You don't realize what you have till it's gone. Do you, Chief?"

"Do you have a picture of Jane?"

The two looked at each other, then shook their heads. Lulu said, "I suppose somebody might have taken pictures at the party, but nobody has shown them to us."

Matthews stood up. "Look folks, I need to talk with my team—my phone's been vibrating in my pocket. I've got a team of eight, they're going to need to eat, and I bet you're willing to provide it. We pay pretty good. Jane, as you call her—and from what you've told me—would want you to profit from this."

He looked out the window. People were lined up on the sidewalk staring at the restaurant and talking behind their hands. "I think there's folks out there that would be willing to tell us why Jane couldn't have killed a man from Missouri. And we want to hear each one of them. So—Clyde, Lulu, would you fry some burgers and fries and make a few salads for my people for lunch?"

Clyde hugged Lulu. "I think he's right. We just need to cooperate. It's what Jane would've wanted. Besides, I think we have five more pies. Lulu, if we don't do it, they'll go somewhere else to eat, then we won't know what's goin' on."

Lulu looked up. "All right then, you make this your command base. Bring in your white board and your gear. "

Matthews grinned. "You been watching cop shows, Lulu? It's settled then. Clyde, I have to ask you one more question. What did you say Jane's last name was?"

"Jones, I think," Clyde said.

"Okay, Clyde, and when was the last time you saw her?"

"I don't rightly know, somewhere around ten o'clock this mornin'. The regular coffee drinkers came in after the breakfast crowd. Oh yeah, she had a nice Chevy pickup. That's where she said she was going—she said she was going to check on her truck."

Matthews got up and said to Clyde, "Show me where she went."

Clyde led Matthews and Blakely through the narrow hallway, past the restrooms, past the door that led upstairs to Jane's apartment, and pointed out the diner's back door.

"Right down that alley, see that garage? That's Baxter's Garage. She probably went there."

Lulu followed and stopped the chief as he turned back around to go up the stairway. She blocked him, putting her hands on her hips. "You're not seeing her apartment until we have a search warrant." She looked at him. "I'm sorry, Chief, but a girl's got to have her privacy. What if she comes back and there you are rummaging through her things?"

৯৬   ৯৬   ৯৬

Matthews checked his watch, followed Blakely into the alley, and ordered, "She's been on the internet, let's see what we can find. Start the process for a search warrant for her apartment and their internet. Find out what Dorney knows and if he's got a BOLO out on her truck. I'll check with the locals, the helicopter crew and roadblocks. Bring the team here—we'd better feed them. It's gonna be a long night. I'll fly back tomorrow and interview Susie Jones and Kate's grandparents."

CHAPTER THIRTY

FOSTER KID

J udge Perkins sat behind his massive oak desk where files were piled high, almost obscuring his view. Behind him, the walls were lined with bookshelves filled with Georgia state statutes. He had a black rotary dial phone on his desk. Next to it sat a newer working phone with several lines.

Perkins studied Blakely over his reading glasses. "You want a warrant to search the apartment of Jane Jones, that little gal from the diner—the one that makes the pies? That is really bad news. Now, tell me again, agent, why do you think this Jane Jones is the woman you're looking for?"

"Sir, she fits the physical description of Kate Anderson. The woman is suspected of killing a deputy sheriff."

"Do you have a picture of this Anderson woman?"

Blakely produced the picture of Kate. "Sir, this is a picture of Kate Anderson, taken approximately two years ago. You can see the resemblance for yourself."

"Well, I don't know, Agent Blakely, it's hard to say. The little gal in the diner didn't wear her hair like this picture. I couldn't say for sure this is the same woman—what makes *you* so sure? I wasn't a regular over to the diner, like a lot of folks in this town, but my secretary brought me food from there a couple times a week. You might ask her if she thinks it's the same woman—oh, I forgot, she took off this afternoon. I think our little gal wore glasses sometimes."

"We've been tracking this woman for eleven months. All roads led to here. The timeline of her appearance in Rebel matches our timeline. Sir, you must admit there is a strong resemblance.

The judge stared at the agent. "What I need is probable cause. What roads led here?"

Blakely started again. "Well, sir, we got a tip from someone that the fugitive was staying at Lulu Harrison's. We need to search her apartment to obtain any clues to where she might have gone."

"How many other tips have you received over the last six months?"

Blakely looked down at his feet. "About twenty credible, and hundreds every day. The family of the victim put out a $300,000 reward."

"According to this affidavit, she was at work this morning, then left. Have you checked the hospital? Maybe she's ill. That young woman never missed work. If I give you this search warrant, and it turns out she's *not* this murdering woman from Missouri—well, she might think we're not a friendly town, and pick up and move." The judge shook his head. "No, no we couldn't have that—the Harrisons depend on that young woman. Have you asked them to search the apartment?"

"Yes sir."

"And, they said, 'no?' Nice folks like that? Hmm. Well, I don't like it. They own the building. There's no crime here. None of my town folk are bleeding. Show me a crime or get me some probable cause for you to snoop in citizens' buildings without any proof. Come see me tomorrow."

"Sir, she could be long gone by then."

"I'm not doin' your job for you, son. I suggest you get back over to the diner and sweet talk Lulu into a search. As far as the computer and the internet, you're wasting your time on me. But, do keep me updated. I want you to see you before you leave town."

❧   ❧   ❧

Blakely opened the door to the diner and sat down at the designated table closest to the kitchen. He liked the Harrisons and had grown increasingly fond of them in the last few days.

"Good morning, Agent Blakely." Lulu poured him coffee. "We'll be closing up right at two o'clock, just like we said."

Mr. Harrison came around from the kitchen, switched the door sign to closed and locked it. "Close enough, to two."

Lulu brought out the luncheon special for the agent: meatloaf, mashed potatoes, green beans. "I made the meatloaf today," Lulu said, "with tomato sauce like it's supposed to be made, not with brown gravy like *he* does."

"Mine's cheaper, and good enough for the men that come in here."

Blakely took a bite. "Oh, this is really good, thank you, Mrs. Harrison."

"See, Clyde?"

"Mine would have been fine."

The agent took another bite. "Yes, sir, but this is mighty tasty."

"Any news regarding our Jane?" Lulu asked.

"Well, yes, ma'am, and I have a few questions. I know you've had dozens of foster children through the years, but do you remember a young girl maybe four or five who you had only a few weeks? She was from Missouri and her parents were killed in a plane crash."

"Kate." Lulu grabbed Clyde's hand. "Oh, my Lordy, it was Kate. It's true. Clyde, our Kate came back to see us—she must've remembered something about us."

Lulu started to cry. Clyde put his arm around his wife and said, "We wanted to adopt that little girl. One day the agency discovered she had a grandfather and just whisked her away. We tried to stay in touch, but never heard from the grandfather. We didn't try to adopt again. Lulu couldn't go through that heartbreak another time."

Lulu looked up, wiped her eyes and said, "Don't get us wrong, we were good *foster* parents, but we became emergency placement only, without ever getting too attached. Every child coming into our home was on temporary loan to us—a temporary blessing."

"Now that you know the connection between Kate and yourself, do you think the woman you called Jane could be Kate Anderson from Missouri?"

Clyde said, "You tricked us. You played on our sympathy and now you are—"

"Clyde, it's not his fault. I understand you're just tryin' to do your job. Can you imagine, Jane was our little Kate?" Lulu started to cry again.

Clyde snatched the plate out from underneath Agent Blakely's fork. "What else do you want with us?"

"Oh, stop it, Clyde. Let the man eat."

Clyde put the plate down.

"Thank you, sir, I'll admit I'm hungry. I'm sorry, I've upset the two of you, but we also need to know if Jane had a boyfriend. Do you know anyone she was seeing?"

"I don't know of anyone, but it was none of our business, was it, Lulu?"

Lulu looked at Clyde. "Well, there was this man—he was in here last week. Clyde, you were over at the barber shop. Jane knew him. He grinned big when he saw her."

"What did he look like?"

"He was a good lookin' fella, kinda looked like Chief Matthews, but younger, shorter. He came in here for a late lunch. He was a bit scruffy, wore a flannel shirt, jeans. Handsome, though. He'd been in here before."

"Please, think, Mrs. Harrison, did he say his name?"

"No, well, I was studyin' them from the kitchen. Jane asked if she could have the rest of the afternoon off. She just got his food to go, he paid, and they left."

They heard a rap on the front door to the café.

Richard Mullen peered through the glass.

"Oh, you might as well see what he wants, Clyde."

Clyde walked to the front door.

"We're closed, Richard."

"I see that—I'm not blind. I found this note in my pocket last night. I forgot I had it. I didn't want to give it to you when the cops were here, but geesh, they're *always* here."

Richard gave the note to Clyde, turned, and walked away. Clyde and Lulu huddled over the paper, then blotted tears from their eyes as they read it together.

Clyde handed the note to Blakely. "It looks like you've got your positive ID."

Blakely looked at it. "I'm not going to take the note into evidence right now, but I'll take a picture with my phone." He snapped the picture and sent it to the forensics team.

"Look folks, I don't mean to intrude. I really don't, but, Mrs. Harrison, would you go up and check Jane's apartment? The judge made a good point. Maybe she *didn't* run, maybe we should be checking hospitals. Would you see if her things are still there?"

Lulu stood up, "Oh, my goodness, yes. I'll go look." She went down the hallway, climbed the steep steps to Jane's apartment, and disappeared for a moment.

"You might as well come up, there's nothing here."

Blakely took the steps two at a time. Entering the room, he scanned the space, and saw a single bed, neatly made with a pink quilted bedspread. The drawers of a tiny dresser with an attached mirror were open and empty. He walked into the bathroom which barely had room for a shower, sink, and toilet.

He opened the closet. Inside was one bare, empty rod.

CHAPTER THIRTY-ONE

REACQUAINTED

S usie rented a loft apartment in the market district in Kansas City, Missouri. Her living room and bedroom had beautiful views of the Missouri River, where at night the casinos, built like old river boats, lit up the night sky. The loft, with its exposed beams and brick walls, was stunning, and was located not far from the Farmer's Market and her job in private security. On Saturdays she frequented her favorite café, The Corner, where yesterday, she had answered the pay phone and spoken to her friend, Kate.

But today, Susie pampered herself as she did every Sunday morning. She drank coffee, read the *Kansas City Star*, then applied a green facial masque and an essential oil treatment for her hair. Her white towel, wrapped around her head turban-style, made her seem three inches taller than her height of six feet. She was barefoot and beginning her pedicure, with her white hotel robe tied loosely at the waist, when her buzzer sounded. Despite the cotton pushed between her toes, she managed to walk over and push the intercom.

"Yes."

"It's Reese Matthews, Susie, buzz me in."

"Commander Reese, I'm not in the mood—and I'm not decent." She took the turban off her head, bent over and shook her blonde mane of hair.

"I'm not leaving, Susie. 'Aiding and abetting a fugitive' is a serious charge."

"You don't scare me, Reese Matthews. Seriously, you can't come up. I'll meet you in an hour."

"At the café with the pay phone?"

"What pay phone?"

"Come to the café in forty-five minutes."

Susie flung her hair into place. *That man. That outrageous, gorgeous man. Threatening me—boy, he knows how to get my engine started.*

She took a quick shower and flat ironed her long hair. She applied eye make-up and lipstick, and then chose a blue silk blouse that matched her eyes. She shimmied into her tightest jeans, rolled at the ankle, and slid on strappy heels.

≪ ≪ ≪

Reese sat in a booth in the back of the café. Another marshal sat at the counter behind which the cook flipped fried eggs next to sizzling bacon and sausage. Reese stood up when Susie walked over to his booth.

She hugged him and kissed him on the cheek, marking him with her lipstick.

"Good morning, handsome." She nodded at the marshal sitting at the counter. "Did you feel the need for back-up?"

"Probably will need it." Reese grinned.

196

"Do I need an attorney? First you threaten me, now you're grinning at me like a monkey."

"Have you done something wrong?"

"I take all threats seriously."

A waitress came over to the table, and they both ordered coffee.

"Where is she, Susie?"

"I've told you a hundred times. I don't know where she is."

"We came pretty close to catching her two days ago."

"Why can't you just drop it, Reese? Just let her go. The guy was a scumbag."

"Susie, you of all people should know I'm trying to save her life. If it were up to me, she'd be back working for me at the Probation Office."

"You're dreaming, if you think *that* would ever happen again."

Reese sipped his coffee and studied Susie. "Did you know Kate bakes delicious pies?"

Susie slapped the table with her palm. "Oh my, Reese, what on earth makes you think Kate can bake? Do you know how ridiculous you sound?" She waited a minute. "Reese, I believe you're blushing. You don't have a positive ID. You came here for some type of confirmation. You won't get it from me."

❧   ❧   ❧

It took only a second for Pete Morrow, Susie's boss, to locate his beautiful employee sitting in a booth with a U.S. marshal. He made eye contact with the agent at the counter. Both calculated a quick threat assessment and then ignored each other.

"Move your butt over, Susie. Who's your friend?"

"Pete Morrow, meet U.S. Marshal, Reese Matthews. He's the one who's been chasing Kate, even though he used to be her boss."

"Morrow." Reese nodded to the man who was taking a seat next to Susie.

"Pete's my boss at Yesterday's Investigations."

"Really, must be quite a business. Tell me about it."

"We mostly run background investigations for local companies. A few private investigations, security assignments. We've been looking for Kate. If we had anything, we'd turn it over to you."

Susie looked at Reese. "We've set up a fund for Kate. I believe she can turn herself in, and we can get her bail money and hire the best attorney. There's a new start-up on the internet. It raises money for good causes. Once she turns herself in, the account will skyrocket. She won't have to spend the night in jail, where she would be killed."

"Good, Susie," said Reese. "Maybe we can combine forces—you show me your stuff and I'll show you mine." He flashed his grin.

Morrow said, "I'd like to see a picture of this woman you thought was Kate. Was she in Georgia?"

"So, you *did* know she was in Georgia."

"No, we probably got the same tip you did. We didn't think it was credible."

"We don't have a picture. Didn't you know that already?" Reese replied.

Susie interrupted the two men. "Kate didn't take one picture of herself? Seems odd. Did you find any fingerprints?"

"No, Susie, we didn't find any prints."

"So, let me interpret this for you, Reese. If she *had* shot that scum, Robert O'Dell, she sure as hell wouldn't have left her fingerprints on her own gun."

"I got it, Susie. I agree with your assessment. Tell me this—why would a simple waitress-baker live in a small Georgian town, get the entire town to love her, save a retired couple from near bankruptcy, and just up and run one morning? She didn't leave *anything* behind. Why would a simple waitress scrub the place clean? Why would she use a name like Jane Jones?"

Susie replied, "Beats me, but we're not wasting our time there. We don't think it was Kate. I think Kate is already in Mexico. She speaks Spanish and with her olive skin—she could sell t-shirts on the beach all day long. She wouldn't still be staying in Georgia."

"Did you give her a fake ID? You have a cousin or sister or somebody that lost an ID?"

Susie laughed, "No, I didn't give Kate a fake ID. I haven't seen Kate. I haven't done any drops for Kate. I haven't seen my friend for almost fourteen months."

Reese waited for Susie to continue.

"Okay, I'll give you one clue, but only if you call me the minute you find her."

"Agreed."

"If Kate left no trace—no clothes, no beauty products—I would be looking into whatever church

199

donation box is available. She wouldn't throw good clothes in a ditch. That's the only lead I'm giving you."

Reese shoved a picture across the table. The picture showed Susie talking on a pay phone.

"It's not a very complimentary photo, Reese. I'd appreciate it if you would keep it for your own private collection." She shoved the picture over to Morrow.

"I'll take a copy, if you're passing them out," Morrow said.

"It's not illegal for me to talk on the phone. The dealer at the antique mall keeps the phone booth active. He thinks it's a novelty. I think it's cute. Use it or lose it—so I use it."

Reese swung out of the booth. "Next time you talk to Kate, tell her to call me." He handed Susie a business card.

"I already have a collection of your cards, Reese."

"This one goes to a burner cell. Have her call me, Susie."

He walked out and the man at the bar followed him.

Morrow looked at Susie. "What do you think?"

"He didn't buy any of it."

CHAPTER THIRTY-TWO

INTERVIEW WITH DYLAN TIMMONS

D ylan Timmons sat in the interview room at the U.S. marshal's office. The entire room was gray—ceiling, table, walls. The window was coated in dust. He walked over to the two-way mirror. "Hey, come talk to me! I've got to get on the road."

I'm nervous—damn, I haven't ever been jammed up like this. Should I call my lawyer? Dang, lawyer'd cost me two thousand bucks and I haven't done anything. They're probably watching me.

On the other side of the window, Matthews and Blakely stared.

Timmons drummed on the table and started singing country songs. *Maybe they'll think I'm nuts.* "I've been every. . . " He lost the words to the song and started another one, still drumming on the table. This time it was Billy Joel. He stood up and pretended to play an air guitar. *I'm nuts, I've gone nuts. I should call my attorney.*

He sat down. When the door began to open, he heard a man yell as he entered the room, "They'll have to wait."

Timmons looked at Matthews, slumped further into the chair, and folded his arms against his chest.

Matthews threw a file on the desk. "You're a busy guy, aren't you?"

Timmons said, "What's this about?"

"You're in some trouble, Timmons, the stuff in this file—petty stuff. County jail time. Now you're in big time trouble. Aiding and abetting a criminal."

"I didn't knowingly aid a criminal. Trust me, I don't *aid* anyone."

Matthews showed Timmons the picture of Kate. "Do you know this woman?"

"Sure, I know Kate. She was a couple years older than me in school. She lived across the street when I was in kindergarten."

Matthews stared and waited. Timmons glared back for a moment, then broke the silence. "My old man used to sweat me like this. Normally, I'd have a staring contest with you, but look, man, I'm a truck driver. I've got to make this haul. I've got a truck payment due. Just ask me your damn questions."

"We're searching for Kate Anderson. She's wanted for murder. When's the last time you saw her?"

"Murder? Kate? C'mon, you're messin' with me. Am I being punked? Where's the camera?"

"Timmons, we know you were seeing her in Georgia."

Blakely knocked on the door. "Sir, would you step outside for a minute?"

Matthews got up from his chair and strode into the hallway. "This better be good, Blakely."

"Sir, you may want to look at the video of the session."

"Why?"

"Sir, you may not be able to see it, but that guy looks like your younger brother. I think he's spotted it."

"What?"

The two moved into the adjoining room and looked through the two-way mirror. Timmons drummed on the table again. Matthews said, "You think *that* guy looks like *me*?"

"Yes, sir. The two of you staring at each other was surreal."

"You take the lead, Blakely."

Blakely opened the door and took a seat. Matthews stood against the wall and studied Timmons.

"Oh great, good cop, bad cop. Look, fellas. I don't know what she's done—I've been a little out of touch with what happens in Kingseat. I've been beaten by cops before—don't need it again. I've got something you want, and I'll be glad to trade for my release."

Blakely turned and looked at Matthews. Neither spoke.

"You can put a tracker on my truck, put a gizmo on my phone. I swear, I don't know where she is. I'm not planning to run into her again. Two days ago, I stopped my truck, went into this little café, and there she was waiting on tables. I'd been to the diner before and knew Lulu. When Lulu saw me talking to Kate, she gave her the afternoon off. We went down by the lake and talked about my folks and her grandparents. She said she was making her way down to Florida. She said she hated being a cop. I couldn't believe my good luck—a woman like that spending time with me. I only saw her once, bro."

Timmons held his hands up in mock surrender. "I'm not reaching for a gun—they searched me. If we have a deal, you let me go. Let me take my load over to Phoenix, and then if you want to ask me more questions, I'll drive my white ass back over here and see you guys." He reached into his pocket, pulled out a strip of pictures, and handed it to Blakely, who studied it. The strip was taken in an old-time photo booth. Kate sat on Timmons' lap, and they were both laughing. Six shots of Kate and Timmons: Kate kissing Timmons on the cheek, Kate with her head back laughing, Kate with her tongue sticking out.

"We took two sets and she gave one to me. She said, 'Hang onto these photos, put them in your pocket close to your heart. It'll be your "get-out-of-jail-free card."' I didn't really believe her, but the truth is, I haven't changed my shirt."

Matthews stared at the pictures. Looking back at him was a younger version of himself, with Kate on his lap.

"Let him go," Matthews said.

Blakely got up to escort Timmons out.

Timmons snickered. "Dude, you've got it bad! Poor bastard." He moved out of arm's reach. "You're never gonna catch her. The only way you'll win this game is if you stop. Maybe she'll come see you some day in the nursing home."

Matthews handed the picture back to Blakely. "She looks so young and happy. Maybe because she's free—and not taking one moment for granted. I thought the people in Rebel were just tight-lipped gypsy rebels. I see now why we had trouble getting a positive ID and a current photo."

Timmons rapped on the door frame. "Look, guys. I really need to get on the road. If you're looking for a murderer, you might want to check into old man Anderson. When I was a kid, we used to hear rumors about Anderson being in the mob. His family came from Italy. I think his businesses were legit—but nobody messed with him. Lots of rumors in Kingseat. Talk to some old-timers at the coffee shop. You know, the plane crash that killed her parents—it might not have been an accident."

CHAPTER THIRTY-THREE

GRANDMA AND GRANDPA

Kingseat, Missouri

Theodore Anderson and his wife Helen sat at their kitchen table watching the snow fly and the neighbor children struggle with their sleds. Theodore's wife had just been released from the nursing home. His thoughts were on how he was going to be able to take care of her with little help from a local nursing agency. *One day at a time.*

"Let's play cards, Helen. The Chiefs' football game will be on later today."

A black SUV pulled into the driveway and the couple looked at each other. "I hope it's not bad news, " Helen said from her wheelchair.

"It's not; they would have called. They're still looking for her."

Matthews stepped out of the vehicle. From his numerous visits to the house, he knew to use the entrance with the sliding glass door off the porch. He took off his white Stetson, and Theodore, seeing him at the sliding door, waved him in.

"Good morning, Mr. and Mrs. Anderson," Matthews said, as he slid the door open. "Chilly day out there."

Dared to Run

"Chief, do you have news about Kate?" Theodore asked.

"Yes, Mr. Anderson, I hate to disturb you, sir."

Mrs. Anderson said, "Oh, it's not really a disturbance, we don't have much company anymore, so it's a welcome distraction on this cold snowy day. Unless it's *bad* news."

"No, it's not bad news, I just wanted to give you an update."

"Liar, " Theodore said.

"Ted, there's no reason to be rude, the man's just trying to do his job."

"He didn't have to take that job to track our Katrina down." Theodore glared at his wife, then at Matthews.

"We're getting off to a bad start. Why don't I tell you what I know?"

Helen pointed at a chair. "Have a seat, Chief. Just lay your hat on that chair in the corner. Would you like a drink? We're starting happy hour early today, because we didn't have Bloody Marys this morning—aren't we, Ted?"

"Are you having one, Mr. Anderson?" Matthews asked.

"I drink Old Crow whiskey and she drinks *her* whiskey, but I've got . . . " He waved his hand in the air . . . "Vodka, scotch— a full bar. How 'bout a beer?"

"Thank you, I'll take a beer."

Theodore got up from the table and opened the refrigerator.

"Looks like all we've got is Budweiser, that's it."

"A Bud would be great."

207

Theodore mixed their drinks as Matthews and Mrs. Anderson discussed her discharge from the nursing home and her plans to live at home.

"I have to wear this damn thing around my neck—I'm a fall risk."

"I think wearing that is a very good idea, Mrs. Anderson."

Theodore set the drink down in front of his wife, placed his hand on her shoulder for a moment, then walked over to get the other drinks. He handed Matthews his beer. "Do you want a glass?"

"No sir, this is fine, thank you. You feelin' all right, Mr. Anderson?" Matthews asked.

"I'm perfect. And now, I have a drink." The old man grinned and winked at his wife. "Tell us what you know, Matthews."

"We followed a lead to a small town in Georgia where a woman fit the description of Kate—Katrina. She worked as a waitress there and everyone seemed to have fallen in love with her, even the local judge. From all accounts, she was in good health and happy, and had been living there about ten months. We confirmed it was Kate."

"Well, that's good news, she's alive, Ted, it's good news."

"Well, of course she's alive. I've never doubted that—she ran off, she didn't go off on some death wish."

"Yes, sir, like I've said each time I've come to your beautiful home, I want to bring her in safely. I think she could beat a murder charge."

"And, I think she better stay on the run—because I didn't raise that girl to be beaten—or kidnapped by some low-life white trash. Of course, she killed him–or she'd be here now—or finishing law school like she was supposed to."

"Ted, you don't know that."

"How many times have you been here, Matthews?" Theodore asked.

"Well, I think this is eleven. Kate brought me here for your anniversary reception, the very first time I met you folks. That was a great party."

"The football game is coming on in half an hour. Is there anything else you were going to tell us?"

"Kate refurbished a pickup truck, but we think she left town on a Harley."

"Well, we don't know anything about that, but Kate was raised driving vehicles and fixing things. She drives about anything. Now—waitressing, that's a different story. You know, Matthews, I think she's in Mexico. Why would she wait around? She studied in Mexico on an exchange program while she was in college. I believe she high-tailed it to Mexico."

"Mr. and Mrs. Anderson, do you remember a couple by the name of Gary and Lulu Harrison?"

"No, I don't think we do—do we, Helen?"

"Evidently, Kate was placed in foster care after her parents' plane went down. She's been helping them the last ten months. Probably saved the couple from bankruptcy."

Helen said, "Oh, yes, we met them. We kept in touch for a short time, but we just stopped replying to them.

It didn't seem like it was helping Katrina. She went and looked them up? Well, that was sweet of her."

Matthews took a sip of his beer, letting the couple take their time and rewind their memories.

"It *was* Katrina, wasn't it, Helen? I had hoped she was in Mexico."

"I think it was, Ted."

"You know, remember that neighbor boy who lived across the street when Katrina was in grade school? I saw him in church—he said he'd seen Kate. What was his name?"

Matthews let the couple talk. He watched the two interact as if lost in their own little world, sipping their whiskey, and trying to remember.

"Timmons—one of those Timmons boys. Dylan maybe. Yes, Larry Timmons' son—lived across the street from us on Morningside."

Reese pulled out a current picture of Kate. "We secured pictures of Kate with Dylan Timmons. I cropped him out and made you folks a copy."

Mr. Anderson took the picture from Matthews. "She does look well, doesn't she, Helen?"

Helen looked at the picture. "I wish she'd come home, Ted."

"She'll come home when it's safe, Helen. We can't lose her, too, like we did her folks."

"You're right, you're so right, Ted."

"I won't be keeping you any longer, but here's my card with a private cell phone number on the back of it. She can call that number—it's not traceable. *You* can call the number, too. Kate's friend, Susie, has a web page that is raising money for attorney fees and bond. I think it's safe for her to come home."

Matthews rose, took his beer bottle, rinsed it in the sink, and walked into the garage to the recycling bin. "Recycling comes tomorrow, Mr. Anderson, can I set your bin out?"

"I'd be much obliged, Matthews, thank you. That bin gets heavy. I'll close the garage door after you." The old man got up from his chair and followed the chief across the kitchen.

"Mrs. Anderson, I'm glad you're home."

"Thank you, for the news and the picture."

Theodore patted Matthews on the back. "Come back, if you hear any news."

Matthews lowered his voice. "Mr. Anderson, one more question. Did you put a hit out on Robert O'Dell?"

"You think I hired a 'hit man' to kill O'Dell with Kate's duty weapon? You think I'd set my own granddaughter up for murder?"

"I'm sorry, I had to ask."

≈ ≈ ≈

Matthews scrolled through his contacts, called Blakely, and started talking as soon as Blakely answered. "I've just come from the Anderson house. Get a tap on Anderson's line. Let's listen to who he talks to. Also, go through his bank accounts. We need to find out if he paid someone to whack Robert O'Dell. Just call the judge."

"Yes, sir. Sir, I've been thinking—she left a clue by the way she left her apartment."

"Go on—I'm listening.

"It certainly looked like she knew we were coming—but, what if she planned to leave all along? She might have shipped her belongings to an undisclosed location. We believe she left on a motorcycle—she didn't take them with her. Shipping places have cameras."

Matthews thought for a moment, then said, "And, with the additional information that she taught the waitress to make pies, it looks like she planned to leave. The more pictures we can get, the better."

"Yes sir. I'm sure you've thought of this—but maybe she looked those people up because she wanted to see them or help them. And, if she shipped her belongings somewhere—she's not randomly running."

"She's checking off items on a bucket list," Matthews said.

"Yes, sir. I think so. I also have been following the leads we've gone through. We've contacted all her old school friends, but—sir, I know it is a long-shot, but we didn't contact the nuns. One of those nuns was only four years older than Kate."

"Blakely, you're a genius."

"Well, thank you sir."

"Kate always had a big-picture plan. Law school— she's heading to a university. Everyone is pointing us south—she's probably headed north. How many people can we get on this?"

"Dorney and a few more to work exclusively on the computer side. We could create a program with her basic information, crosscheck it with law schools, and narrow it down from there. The deadline for the January sessions has probably expired. We might be able to generate a new lead."

"I'll go interview the nuns—right after I have a drink at Dirty Sally's."

CHAPTER THIRTY-FOUR

REASONABLE DOUBT

Kingseat, Missouri
August 13, 2015 — Three years later

A little before dawn Kate, dressed in camo fatigues, climbed a large oak tree in the field near the McCown Funeral Home, and settled in with her binoculars. Her tan arms and face blended into the tree. She added a field hat to corral her dark brown hair. *This makes me invisible.*

Her thoughts turned to her grandfather, who had remembered her instructions. "Pops, if you need me to come home, place an ad in the *Kansas City Star* classifieds on a Saturday that reads, 'Matilda, call home.' I'll find a paper every week."

When Kate saw the ad published one weekend, she called Pops on his home phone. He delivered the grave news. "Ron Davis passed away."

Without hesitation, Kate had replied, "Pops, I'm coming home, I'm turning myself in. I might not make bail. I'll be a flight risk, but I need to see you and grandma—and I have to pay my respects to Ron."

The funeral would start at ten a.m.—a long wait. Later today, she planned to turn herself into the

Livingston County Sheriff's Department, two counties away. She could not risk being captured in Chariton County by the deputies employed by Sheriff O'Dell. Her planned escape route drummed in her mind until the sun broke through the early morning sky in shades of pink and orange.

She heard a twig snap and sat like a statue, the urge to move almost unbearable. A man dressed in dark navy approached, searching for footprints or any trace of the fugitive. She recognized the man as Steve Blakely, lead investigator for the U.S. marshal's office. In the last few years, Blakely had muscled up.

He lives up to his name, "Bulldog." I'm invisible. Don't move a muscle.

Blakely stopped a moment under the oak tree and scanned the area.

I should turn myself in, right here, right now, give Blakely the credit for finding me. Maybe they would take me to the fed jail and not the county jail. Kate smiled. *But then I would miss paying my respects and . . . the fun.*

Blakely moved on, scanning the ground. He crossed the fence into the cemetery. Kate watched the "U.S. Marshal" white lettering on his jacket shine in the morning sun and fade as he moved away.

She gave a small sigh of relief. *Stick with the plan. I doubt he will check again.* She picked up her binoculars and checked for more agents. A man, dressed in a green jump suit and raking leaves, caught her attention. *Who wears green jump suits in Kingseat, Missouri?* Kate chuckled. *There's agent number two.* She looked for Matthews and for more agents.

A few minutes later, she found herself lost in thought about the man who would be buried today. *What will I do without you in this world? You always believed in me. You were my true American hero—my brother, my friend, my compass. How can you be gone?*

Kate fought back tears.

৵   ৵   ৵

The McCown Funeral Home was located at the edge of town, with the cemetery conveniently behind it. Forty acres of cut hay left room for expansion of the cemetery for future use.

Matthews had orchestrated a team of eight U.S. marshals along with eight local law enforcement agents, even though he didn't trust any of the local team. Kate had her supporters, but she also had enemies. To some of these officers, she had killed one of their own—in cold blood—execution style.

C'mon, Kate. Just turn yourself in. I can protect you.

Reverend Amos Cook conducted the service. The room was filled with people dressed in black, except for the two rows of seats marked "Reserved" behind the family. These rows remained empty.

Four federal agents in navy blue blazers, tan pants and blue ties, stood at the front of the four aisles. Their badges were clipped to their lapel pockets, and covered with a black ribbon, showing respect for their fellow officer, Ron Davis.

At 9:59 a.m. six women arrayed in long curly blonde wigs proceeded down the aisle. They all wore identical black short skirts and lowcut lacy tops. Whispers and giggles erupted throughout the room as the mourners realized Dolly Parton impersonators were entering the chapel. Everyone knew Ron had been a Dolly fan. Each look-alike carried a red rose and walked procession-style down to the second row of seats—step, pause, step, pause. Reese studied the tallest woman, well over six feet in height. *Susie—what in the hell are you up to?*

The U.S. marshals scanned the women's faces and then their bodies, checking for a woman who was five-foot six. Adjusting for the height of their shoes, five women fit that description.

A few seconds later, a procession of six women dressed in gothic attire entered the church. Their white faces stood out against black lipstick and overdrawn eyebrows. Each wore square rimmed glasses, their black hair done up in pigtails and spider bows. These women wore boots to their knees and were all the same height.

Whispers crackled through the funeral home.

A U.S. marshal's photographer carefully snapped pictures of the twelve women. Each stared directly at the camera and posed for the shot. The photos would be run through a facial recognition program. Because they were attempting to match one face, it wouldn't take long.

The marshals touched their earpieces, listening to an order from Matthews. "Stand down, wait."

Reverend Amos Cook stood up and walked to the podium. "We are here today to celebrate the life of Ron Davis. This ceremony will be brief in accordance with the instructions he left. I will read his last words, then we will proceed to the cemetery where there will be a military burial.

"As you can all see, Ron had a great sense of humor. We can all smile as we think of him and welcome his guests who have traveled here today. Obviously, 'they aren't from around here.'"

The crowd laughed nervously.

"If I'm not mistaken, we have a celebrity in the house: the famous 'Just Dollie,' star of the Country Jamboree from Branson."

All eyes turned to the Dolly Parton impersonators. Susie stood up, turned to the crowd, waved and sat down. Reverend Cook continued. "As you can all see, we have U.S. marshals in the building. They are searching for the fugitive, Kate Anderson. Please give them your full cooperation."

The reverend paused, waiting for the crowd to settle into their seats. The whispering continued. He spread his arms wide, his white and gold robe hanging from his arms, and the crowd quieted. "And now words from Navy Chief Davis." Reverend Cook stood a little taller, picked up the speech and read:

I love this country. As a young man of eighteen, I joined the Navy. I was blessed to have been accepted into one of the most prestigious units on earth. As a Navy Corpsman I met and assisted the bravest young men in the world. I was lucky enough to be promoted up the ranks and given the opportunity to see the world. I have had the comradery of the finest men.

218

The reverend gazed at Davis's family and continued.

I love my small community and my family. Even when I was not with you, I loved you. I hope you will live a full, true life and be the best you can be.

Cook looked over at Matthews.

I wanted my family, my wife and friends to learn this from me. I've sent a confession to the sheriff admitting to shooting Robert O'Dell. Sometimes monsters need be taken out of this world.

A communal gasp rose from the mourners. Conversations broke out.

Matthews studied the women in the pews. Three of the ladies dressed in black huddled with their heads together.

Reverend Cook waved his hands over his head. "Excuse me, excuse me, let's get the man buried. Then, we can all jaw about this over the dinner in the church hall."

Half the crowd ignored him.

"Please, let me finish!" He picked up Davis's speech and began reading again:

I am a soldier—and it was something I could do for this community. I hope God and you will forgive me.

The reverend paused, looked up into the choir loft, and motioned for the soloist to begin "Amazing Grace." He waved the ushers to their stations.

The ushers moved to the front of the church and the first row of family members exited out the front aisle during the song. After the family left the chapel, the twelve women exited out the side aisle, without the benefit of the usher. Several people swarmed "Just Dollie" for autographs. The funeral home turned into a traffic jam.

❧   ❧   ❧

Matthews hadn't expected the unusual exit by the twelve women. He also hadn't expected the congregation to move toward the women or ask for autographs. He made his way through the crowd and announced, "U.S. Marshal, stand back." He wove through the crowd to the tall blonde.

Susie looked up from signing an autograph. "Hello, handsome."

"Where's Kate?"

"Honey, I'm not sure where she is right now, but this note has been passed to me and I believe it's for you. A little bit like grade school, isn't it, Doll?"

She handed him the message.

Hello Reese, you're looking good—all tall, dark and handsome in your U.S. marshal's blue blazer. I'm turning myself in. Please meet me at the Livingston County Sheriff's Office. I'll get better treatment there.

Davis's confession gives me reasonable doubt, but we both know he didn't shoot O'Dell. He'd never set me up for a murder charge.

See you soon, Kate

Reese said, "I should arrest you, Susie."

"Honey Doll, I have bail money, take me in." Susie reached into her abundant cleavage and pulled out a roll of one-hundred-dollar bills. "Do you want to see the other roll?"

❦   ❦   ❦

Dorney stopped the eleven women and asked for identification, then allowed them to leave in two limos waiting for them. He reported, "I only count eleven. She may still be in the building."

❦   ❦   ❦

As local law enforcement officers, mixed with marshals, searched the funeral home, five more cars pulled up, lining the road to the burial site. Twenty-five more women, dressed in black, got out of the cars and joined the ceremony.

The military service was heart-wrenching and beautiful. The first volleys of rifle fire shocked the crowd. Women put their hands over their hearts until the volleys stopped. A young man stood tall as he played taps. Mourners wiped their eyes as a young marine kneeled in front of Davis's widow and handed her his flag. His three children stood behind her. The youngest looked like a miniature Ron Davis.

ॐ   ॐ   ॐ

The procession of family and friends walked out of the cemetery. Agents moved with the crowd. Radios crackled back and forth, but no one had eyes on the fugitive.

"Follow the cars," Matthews barked over the radio. "Blakely, stay with me." The two retraced their steps to the funeral home, where Matthews spotted a cellar door standing wide open. He ran toward the cellar, but then stopped and glanced back at the grave site. There, a woman stood in gothic attire. A black lacy parasol twirled over her shoulder, and she blotted her eyes.

Matthews yelled, "Kate! Stop!"

The woman dropped her parasol and ran. Ripping off a black wrap-around skirt, she threw it into the air and sprinted toward the hayfield. Blakely ran after her, with Matthews close behind. She zigzagged through the gravestones and leaped over a barbed wire fence like a deer running for freedom, then headed straight into the open field.

Blakely, laden down by his heavy police gear, stopped at the fence.

A small crop duster plane taxied into the field and rolled straight for the runner. It swiveled, made a U-turn, and started in the opposite direction. Kate ran with the aircraft and scrambled into it.

Blakely pulled his service revolver and pointed at the plane. Matthews grabbed his arm a second before he could fire a shot. "Don't shoot!"

J.J. Clarke

QUESTIONS AND TOPICS
FOR DISCUSSION

1. Do you know anyone who was involved in a domestic violence relationship? What happened to them?
2. What could have Kate done differently— besides run? What do you believe the outcome would have been?
3. Is the concept of the underground network of women believable?
4. Did you want more about the romance between Reese and Kate?
5. Are you wondering if Kate had a child?
6. Why did the author pick the quote at the beginning of the book?
7. Do you want more Kate Anderson mysteries?

8. The author intended this book to be a nice break from your regular book club reads. Did it achieve that purpose?

9. There are three missing years in the novel. Would you like to see where Kate went and what happened to her?

TURN THE PAGE FOR AN EXCERPT

Kate Anderson, now a highly successful journalist, receives a desperate call from her grandfather, a victim of the town's white-collar crime organization.

Drugged and put in a nursing home against his will, Pops turns to the one person he can rely on to fight for him and make the bad guys pay. A novel of friendship, grit, and hope, *Dared to Return* will have you cheering once again for Kate and her friends as they unravel the sinister secrets of this thriving town.

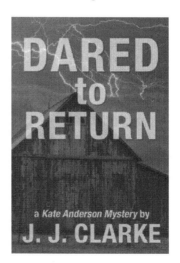

J.J. Clarke

EXCERPT FROM DARED TO RETURN

CHAPTER ONE

POPS

Tampa, Florida, September 2015, 11:30 pm

K ate Anderson's phone buzzed. She stopped pedaling the elliptical in the Anytime Fitness Center. The machine slowed to a stop and she glanced at her watch.

"Pops, is that you?"

"Katrina, Oh, Katrina, thank goodness I reached you — please come home."

"What's wrong, Pops? You never call me this late." Kate stepped off the machine, crossed the gym floor, wiped her forehead with a towel and strained to hear her grandfather's voice.

"Katrina, I don't want to stay here."

Kate pushed open the locker room door and froze. A cold chill crept down her spine and crawled up her forearms.

"Where are you, Grandpa? What's wrong?"

"I'm at Squaw Valley Nursing Home. They moved me here."

"What — I mean, who? Grandpa, who moved you there? Why aren't you home? Are you ill?"

"No, no, I'm not sick — that trustee. I can't remember his name — it doesn't matter. I must go. They are looking for me. Please come home, Katrina."

"Pops!" Katrina heard the click on the other end of the line and stared at her phone. Kate immediately hit redial. He did not answer. *Who can I call? Surely, there's someone I can call.* She wiped imaginary sweat from her brow.

What's happened since Grandma's funeral? How has he gone from their home to a nursing home in just four or five weeks? Kate pressed the travel app on her phone, booked a flight, a rental car and a hotel. *When was the last time I talked to him? Grandma's funeral? How long has it been since the funeral, four, five weeks? How can he be in a nursing home? Trustee, what trustee?*

Kate reached up and felt her cheeks as they flushed in anger. *This can't be happening. I just want to scream!* Kate's relationship with her grandfather had always been strained, but family duty trumped everything.

Kate jogged down the steps, out of the gym and to her car. She cursed that she had parked at the far end of the parking lot underneath the light. Her red Mazda's lights blinked a few seconds before she arrived. She slid into the driver's seat, started the engine and then sped through town, blowing a few stop signs.

❧   ❧   ❧

Kate arrived at her luxury one-bedroom apartment overlooking Tampa Bay. She grabbed a suitcase from the closet and packed a few clothes. Cosmetics and hair clips laid neatly lined up in the drawer and ready to be put into her cosmetic bag. Years of practice paid off— and the items flew into her case. *Still on the run.* The irony played on the corner of her mouth and she smiled, loving the adrenaline. Once at the airport, she fired a text to her friend and publicist.

Hey girl, jetting out tonight.
Pops needs me.
Reschedule my book club signings.
Gotta run to catch a flight.
Kate.

A text bubble burst onto Kate's phone.
Oh, no you don't. Not this time.
Text me the details. I'll meet you there.

❧   ❧   ❧

Will Johnson, the plane's steward, waited for the remaining passenger to board. Why can't people just get on the damn plane? It looks like another boring flight. He looked at his watch. His last passenger had another two minutes. He saw her walking up the ramp, dressed in designer jeans and a leather jacket. Her long brown hair, braided French style, pulled away from the face. She wore tall expensive leather boots and walked like a model. She carried a large Coach handbag. When she reached him, she gave him her ticket.

"Good evening, Ms. Anderson. I'm glad you made it. My name is Will and I'm your attendant. Your seat is the first one on the left."

"First-class, I like it." Kate tossed her bag into the compartment and crumpled into the first seat across from where the steward sits facing the passengers. She buckled her seatbelt. The plane was warm and dark. She reached up to add air from the port above her seat and wriggled out of her coat.

Will walked the aisle, checked passengers' seat belts and closed overhead compartments. *Wow. My night just got more interesting.*

Most passengers were settling in for the night flight nap. The plane was only half full and dimly lit. He returned to his little jump-seat facing Kate and buckled himself.

"I've been drinking," Kate announced. "I always say that when I've had one too many." She laughed and shook her head. "I sped all the way here, well I always speed. I didn't know they had those little convenience stores with alcohol."

Will leaned toward the beautiful woman. "You're not afraid of flying? It's the safest transportation."

"I'm not afraid." Kate massaged the palms of her hands and then her fingers. "It's more like dreadful memories. My parents were killed in a plane crash when I was four."

"No— now you're kidding, right?"

"My father piloted the plane carrying the newly elected U.S. Senator, my small town's claim to fame. It crashed at the airport in Kingseat, Missouri."

"Wow, yes, flying must be hard, but your ticket was changed to first-class, so you must fly often."

"No, my business partner is a frequent flyer. I'm sure she changed my ticket." Kate held her breath as the plane released the brakes and started down the runway.

"You know the best thing for you to do is to take big breaths — and let's talk — it will be a good diversion."

"Sounds good — talk, Will. Tell me your story. I'm a writer in desperate need of a new story." Kate closed her eyes for a moment. *I wonder if my mother was terrified the night she died.*

"Don't go to sleep, Kate. Yes, I'll tell you my story."

Kate opened her eyes and studied the young man. "How old are you, Will?"

"I remember the story of your parent's plane crash, so I am a few years older than you, thirty-two. I'm a licensed engineer -- graduated six years ago from the University of Missouri. I'm working on my master's in business. I applied for this job right out of college as a lark. I love to fly — I wanted to be a pilot — but my depth perception is poor. I am, however, the exact right height to close these bins." He pointed upward and shot her a little grin. "The job gives me a great deal of freedom and — and at least I might have adventures to tell my grandchildren someday. Right now, I fly Tampa to Kansas City and live in K.C."

The plane began the ascent and Kate grabbed the arms of her chair.

"It's really okay. Anyway, that's my life story — *Cliff* note style. Tell me more about yourself. When the seat belt sign goes off, I'll get you another drink."

Kate readjusted in her seat and took a deep breath. "Let me see, my story— well, it's a little complicated. I grew up in Kingseat, Missouri, raised by my grandfather, step grandmother and a nanny — a sweet Amish lady. It took all of them, I was a wild child. I went to Catholic school, graduated from college with a law enforcement degree, worked as a bond investigator until five years ago. I planned to go to law school, but instead— fled after becoming the prime suspect in a murder investigation.

Will sat up taller in his seat, his mouth fell open and he stared at the woman sitting across from him. He managed to say, "This time you *are* joking?"

Kate grinned. "Oh, that margarita really loosened my tongue. I wish I were joking. A warrant was issued for my arrest and instead of turning myself in and sitting in jail convicted of a crime I didn't commit, I kept moving, barely a step ahead of the U.S. Marshall's Office." Kate shrugged her shoulders. "No big deal really. Like you said—adventures to tell the grandchildren."

"You aren't on the run now, are you?" Will asked with a crooked little smile.

Kate did not return his smile, but instead looked out the window. Suddenly she turned and brightened, lighting up the dark plane. "No, crazy, I couldn't fly if I had a warrant out for me."

"You should write a book."

"I did. It's called *Dared to Run*, not exactly a best seller, but we have a marketing plan. I work a few private investigations and write articles for blogs and a few newspapers. Like you said, it works for me. Oh, and—my partner is a pretty successful Youtuber."

"Wow, what kind of Vlog? Business partner, right? Not partner, like in a relationship partner."

"It's based on the 1920's gentlemen's club entertainment, just a little burlesque show, you know — beautiful women, great bodies, a little skit making fun of modern times, and a little skin. We say we are artsy, not nudey. It's a little risqué. Susie's the star–I write the skits."

"I keep saying, you're joking, right?"

"No, that's me. Condensed version. Oh, yes, I'm single."

Will got up and pointed toward the front deck. "I need to make sure my partner has the bar cart. She'll cover for me. Hold your thought, we're not done. Can I get you something? A drink, pretzels, chips?"

"Water, please, coffee later. I have a long drive when we land."

Will returned to his seat across from Kate. She was busy making notes in a small spiral notebook.

"Almost everyone's asleep, so I can talk. Kate, do you live in Tampa?"

"Yes, I love it here. I'm flying in to Missouri to check on my grandfather. He asked me to come home, so here I am, on a plane. It might turn into an extended stay. I feel guilty." Kate stopped herself and shook her head. "Why am I telling you this? You probably didn't want to hear my confession."

"You have my full attention, confess away."

"My grandmother died about five weeks ago. I should have stayed after the funeral. I've been busy promoting my book, building a new life for myself. Now that I think about it, my grandfather was pushing me out the door, hiding something. I should have known better."

Kate shifted in her seat. "Let's change the subject. Do you know you look like JFK?"

"Of course, people tell me that all the time." Will laughed at himself. "I'm joking. Well, a couple of times. Once, a woman said to me, 'are you Jack Kennedy?' The two laughed. "I don't know what she was thinking," Will said.

He cocked his head at Kate. "You look like…hmm … I don't know, this might get me in trouble."

"I'll help you out, this is my standard 'Sandra Bullock, don't approach me' look. Do you see it?"

"I spotted it immediately when you were coming up the ramp, not so much now."

"My friends know I'm much like her character in Miss Congeniality."

The two laughed and whispered secrets in the darkness, creating their own private world until it was time to land. When the plane started its descent, Will moved over next to Kate and held her hand. She placed her head on his shoulder and closed her eyes.

ABOUT THE AUTHOR

J. J. Clarke, author of the Kate Anderson Mysteries, *Dared to Run* and *Dared to Return*, spent her career in the State of Missouri as an investigator, parole officer, and administrator of the largest penitentiary in the state. Clarke draws on her extensive experience in law enforcement and her degree in psychology to craft compelling characters and stories. Her heroines are fearless, funny and tenacious.

Clarke and her husband Barry Johnson are restoring a heritage farm in Missouri, and support family businesses and entrepreneurs. They live most of the time in Florida where she is a member of the Florida Writers' Association and local writers' groups.

"I hope my books are entertaining and thought-provoking. I wrote them for book clubs—weekend beach reads with topics for discussion that promote engaged conversation."

Clarke loves to hear from her readers. Please contact her through her website email at JJClarkeAuthor.com and follow her on Facebook and Goodreads.

Made in United States
Orlando, FL
05 July 2022

19435118R00139